SCARY SEA STORIES

VOL. 2

By Mark Kehl

Interior illustrations
by Michael Ellison

ROXBURY PARK

LOWELL HOUSE JUVENILE

LOS ANGELES

NTC/Contemporary Publishing Group

Published by Lowell House
A division of NTC/Contemporary Publishing Group, Inc.
4255 West Touhy Avenue, Lincolnwood (Chicago), Illinois 60712-1975 U.S.A.

Lowell House books can be purchased at special discounts when ordered in bulk for premiums and special sales. Contact Department CS at the following address:

NTC/Contemporary Publishing Group
4255 West Touhy Avenue
Lincolnwood, IL 60712-1975
1-800-323-4900

ISBN: 0-7373-0400-6
Library of Congress Catalog Card Number: 98-66684

Roxbury Park is a division of NTC/Contemporary Publishing Group, Inc.

Managing Director and Publisher: Jack Artenstein
Editor in Chief, Roxbury Park Books: Michael Artenstein
Director of Publishing Services: Rena Copperman
Editor: Rachel Livsey
Editorial Assistant: Nicole Monastirsky
Interior Designer: Victor Perry
Interior Illustrations: Michael Ellison
Cover Art: Mike Harper

Printed and bound in the United States of America
99 00 01 DHD 10 9 8 7 6 5 4 3 2 1

CONTENTS

Overboard

5

Nature's Revenge

22

The Lighthouse

37

The Mermaid's Kiss

56

The Off-Season

70

Island of Terror

86

Shell Raiser

99

Blackheart's Treasure

113

OVERBOARD

I didn't want to go from the start. The cruise was Mom's idea, a way to celebrate their 15th wedding anniversary. So why did I have to go? I wasn't even born 15 years ago.

Because Mom and Dad didn't trust me to stay home by myself. That's what it came down to. So, okay, I'd gotten into a little trouble with my friends: Mario, Chopper, Zach, Chuckie, and Lee. We called ourselves the Deere Street Demons, because we all lived on Deere Street, except for Chuckie, but he only lived one block over and his parents had a pool, so we let him join the gang. We called it a gang, but it wasn't really. I mean, we didn't all wear the same color or sell drugs or anything. We just hung out together. But still, people got the wrong idea, which is why we were banned from the Cloverleaf

Shopping Center. We didn't do anything but hang around and ride our skateboards. We were good customers, spending money at the convenience store on soda and candy bars and stuff. Of course, we probably stole more than we bought, but *they* never knew that. We never got caught.

At least, we never got caught shoplifting. Okay, the cops did nail us the time we set that vending machine on fire. And also the time we stole CDs and change out of unlocked cars over on Carlton Avenue. But I didn't do any of that. It was Chopper who torched the vending machine, and Zach and Mario who took stuff from the cars. It wasn't me. It wasn't my idea. I was just there. Sure, I knew the stuff they were doing was wrong, but what was I supposed to do? Tell them to stop? They were my friends. If I didn't go along with it, they wouldn't let me hang out with them. Mom and Dad just didn't understand.

So they wouldn't trust me to spend one week at home by myself. They thought my friends were a bad influence and it would be good for me to spend some time away from them. That's how I ended up on the cruise.

I tried to make the best of it. I mean, it does sound sort of cool, right? Sailing around the ocean on a boat the size of a shopping mall. But there was nothing to *do*. I explored the ship, but kids weren't allowed in any of the really cool places, like the casinos and nightclubs and the hallways with doors marked CREW ONLY. There was a video arcade, but all the games were old and stupid. I tried to go swimming, but each of the pools had about a hundred people packed in them. I was really bored.

I couldn't even enjoy a chilly soda, because they charged your room three bucks a bottle, and Dad said that was too outrageous. So I hung out by the bar next to the pool, where they kept sodas cold in a big tub of ice. When the bartender was busy, I sneaked back there and helped myself to a couple. Two was more than I needed, but why not? They were free.

That's when I saw this kid sitting on a deck chair and playing a video game. He was littler than I was, but he had the new Scream Team game. I went over to him and offered him one of the sodas if he'd let me play.

"Cool," he said. "You know what they charge for these things?"

"Yeah, it's a rip-off," I told him. "But what are you supposed to do? Get off the boat and walk to a convenience store? My name's Brad."

His was Louis. From Rhode Island. He was only 10, but he was funny and he had the latest versions of all the best video games. We played and hung out there on deck all afternoon, talking about where we were from and our friends and about TV shows. Stuff like that. It was actually pretty fun.

When our sodas ran out, a waiter came by, took the empties, and asked if we wanted more. I shook my head, but after he left, I said to Louis, "Check this out."

I headed across the deck, winding my way through the deck chairs and umbrella-covered tables back to the bar area. It was busier than ever, and I had no problem scoring two more sodas. I headed back to Louis and handed him one.

"You *stole* these?" he said, staring at the can like it might explode.

"Hey," I said, "as much as our moms and dads paid for this cruise, they owe us a few drinks. Enjoy."

He did, but it was obvious my stealing bothered him. It wasn't until 10 or 15 minutes later that we were talking as before. I didn't want to scare him off or anything—we still had six days left on this boat—so I decided I wouldn't do anymore stealing.

And I wouldn't have, if it hadn't been for Tony.

THE SHIP HAD this big, glitzy theater with a stage and a balcony where they put on live shows at night. But during the day they would pull down a giant screen and show movies. The second day they were showing the latest Galaxy Battleship movie. After spending the morning playing Ping-Pong, Louis and I decided to go check it out. That's where we met Tony.

He was my age but bigger. He had curly brown hair and a Chicago accent, and he could do near-perfect impressions of just about anyone in any of the Galaxy Battleship movies. We discovered this about halfway through the movie and put him through his paces. We'd already seen the movie before so we didn't care if we missed any of it.

"Do Jojo Bar," Louis whispered.

"So, a warrior you want to be," Tony said loudly in the requested voice. "First, my butt you must kiss."

We were laughing so hard at his impressions that we didn't notice the crewperson until she was right in front of us, asking us to leave. Tony howled like Chewie, and then we left, still laughing.

TONY REMINDED ME a lot of Chopper. The Deere Street Demons didn't really have a leader, but Chopper was the closest we had. He was the biggest and the loudest of us all, and whatever he wanted to do is what we did.

After we got kicked out of the movie, we hung out on deck for a while. Tony was a huge science fiction fan. He had seen every movie or TV show that Louis or I could name and knew all the actors' names too. He even had autographs from a lot of the stars because he went to sci fi conventions. He was pretty cool.

So when Tony said he was going to order himself a drink, I told him not to bother and headed for the bar. With him and Louis watching, I struck again. I probably could have stolen three colas, but one in each hand was easier. I didn't want to accidentally drop one and get caught. I gave one to Tony and opened the other myself. I didn't look at Louis, but after a minute he left to get himself a cup of water.

Tony and I played Louis's video game for a while. Louis never got a turn to play because, as Tony pointed out, "It's your game—you get to play it all the time." I felt kind of bad for Louis, but I wasn't going to say anything and get Tony mad at me.

Once we tired of the game, we spent the rest of the after-noon prowling the ship. We saw a few doors marked CREW ONLY. Because Tony was curious, we looked to see what was behind them. Tony opened the first door. A foreign-looking guy was feeding dirty bed sheets into a big machine.

"You no come in here," the man shouted over the noise of the machine.

Tony closed the door. "You no come in here," he said, nailing the man's accent his first try. We laughed as we walked down the hallway.

At the next CREW ONLY door, Tony said it was my turn to open it. I didn't really want to do it. We didn't get in trouble the first time, but with my luck it would be the captain standing on the other side of this door. But I wasn't going to back down in front of Tony, so I grabbed the handle and opened the door.

Behind it was a large kitchen with all stainless-steel walls and floors and with pots and pans hanging everywhere. To one side, a woman dressed all in white was chiseling a block of ice the size of a washing machine. She hadn't gotten very far, but it looked as if she were carving an elephant. When she looked up, I waved and backed out. She just smiled. It wasn't so bad.

Still, when we found a third CREW ONLY door and Tony said it was Louis's turn to open it, Louis said he didn't want to.

"Don't be a baby," Tony told him.

Louis looked at me. It wasn't a very fun game, and we probably would get in trouble sooner or later. But Tony was looking at me too, so there was only one thing I could do. "Come on," I said. "We both did it. It's your turn."

Tony nodded approvingly. "Yeah, come on. You're not chicken, are you?"

But Louis was saved when Tony happened to look down and saw something on the floor. "Look!" he said, grabbing it. Louis and I moved closer to see what he'd found.

"It's a casino token," Tony said. "One buck."

"But kids aren't allowed in the casino," Louis pointed out. "How are you going to cash it in?"

"I'm not going to cash it in," Tony said. "We're going to gamble it."

WE MANAGED TO sneak into the casino when no one was looking, and Tony slipped the token into a slot machine. It whirred for a minute and then stopped. Nothing else happened, so we figured we lost. One of the crew noticed us then and chased us out.

It was time to get ready for dinner, but we made plans to meet afterward. Louis wanted to play Ping-Pong, but Tony said Ping-Pong was for wusses. We would find something else to do.

After Tony headed off, Louis followed me. After a few seconds, he said, "Maybe we shouldn't meet Tony after dinner."

I glanced at him. "Why not?"

He shrugged. "My parents will be out. We could stay in my cabin and play cards and watch TV. There'll probably be a movie on."

"And what? Just not tell Tony?"

He shrugged again. Part of me was tempted, but Louis was just some geeky 10-year-old. Tony, with his funny voices and his knowledge of science fiction, was cool. It really wasn't much of a choice.

"I don't think so," I said.

WHEN I WENT to meet Tony after dinner, I wasn't expecting to see Louis, but there he was. We hung out on deck for a while and then went down to look in the nightclubs and make fun of people dancing. When we got tired of that, we just walked around the ship, looking for something to do.

It was windy outside on the upper decks. The ocean stretched out forever into the night. Even though the moon was out, it was on the other side of the ship so our side was dark and shadowy. We stopped to look over the rail. Lights shone through windows and portholes beneath us. We could hear the mighty rush of water as the ship thrust itself through the ocean, but we couldn't see the water in the blackness below.

That's when Tony climbed over the rail. He turned around so his heels were still on the deck. Then, with his hands holding the rail behind him, he extended his arms so he was hanging out away from the ship. There was nothing between him and the dark water below.

"What are you doing?" I gasped. Just thinking about hanging off the ship gave me a lightheaded feeling, as if I were already falling.

"What's it look like I'm doing?" Tony snapped. "Come on, you've got to try it. It's like flying."

Louis and I looked at each other. I guess he wasn't any more thrilled about it than I was.

"Come on," Tony implored. "What are you, chicken?"

If only I had listened to Louis and spent the evening in his parents' cabin I wouldn't be in this horrible mess. This was dangerous and I didn't want to do it, but I was afraid Tony would make fun of me if I didn't. As I climbed over, I kept both hands locked around the rail as if trying to strangle it. Then I turned around and faced away from the ship like Tony. The sensation was so terrifying I could barely move.

"Come on, Louis," Tony ordered impatiently.

"Yeah," I said, laughing nervously, "don't be a loser, Louis."

Tony laughed appreciatively at that. He let go with one hand and clapped me on the shoulder. I couldn't even look at him, hanging by one hand.

Louis climbed carefully over the rail and made it to the other side next to me. He hugged the rail tightly and refused to look down.

"Now turn around," Tony commanded. Leaning outward as he was, he could see right past me to where Louis clung to the rail. "That's the whole point."

"Come on," I said, "you aren't chicken, are you?" I don't even know why I said it. To keep my mind off falling, I guess.

Louis shot me an accusing look as if this were all my fault, and then he looked down at his feet. He swung one

leg around as he turned, but his heel slipped off the edge of the deck. He dropped, his arms stretched to their full length, and then he lost his grip. Louis plunged past the lighted portholes below us and then vanished into the darkness. Over the noise of the ship tearing through the ocean, we didn't even hear the splash.

I QUICKLY BUT carefully hauled myself back over the rail. I didn't know whether to shout or run. Tony followed and grabbed me by the arm.

"What are you doing?" he asked.

"Louis," I said. "We have to tell someone."

"No, we don't." Tony said quietly. I guess I was still looking in all directions, because he grabbed my shirt with both hands and shook me so hard my teeth clacked together. "Listen to me," he commanded, speaking in a low, hard voice, his face inches from mine. "We're not going to tell anyone about this."

"But," I objected, looking over my shoulder at the ocean. "Louis. We have to go back for him. Send boats to search for him."

Tony forced me to look at him again. "There's no point. The fall would have killed him. Do you hear me? It's too late for rescues. Louis is dead."

"Oh, God," I said, trying to find some way not to believe it.

"He's gone," Tony said, "but it was an accident, right? There's no reason for us to get in trouble."

I nodded. It was an accident.

"So here's what we're going to do: nothing."

"Nothing?" I asked, not getting it.

"That's right. Look, lots of people saw us with Louis tonight, but no one saw what happened. After Louis's parents miss him, someone will come ask us about him. It's 10 o'clock now. So we just say that we got tired around 10 and all went our separate ways. We don't know where Louis went after that. They'll search the ship, but they won't find him. They'll think he must have fallen overboard, which is the truth. It's too bad, but there's no reason we should get in trouble, right? Right?

IT TOOK ME forever to fall asleep that night. I kept expecting Louis's parents and the ship's captain to come question me. And when I finally got my mind off that, all I could think about was what it would feel like to slip and fall 12 stories through the darkness, dropping so fast that hitting the water would be like landing on concrete.

I woke up the next morning hoping the whole thing had been a bad dream, but I knew it wasn't. My parents asked if I were feeling all right. I told them I was tired from staying up too late the night before. Then we went up on deck for breakfast.

The ship had arrived at our first port of call, the island of St. John. As we passed through the breakfast buffet line, my parents asked if I wanted to go ashore with them. To their surprise, I said yes. At least on shore I wouldn't have to worry about the captain tapping me on the shoulder to ask about Louis.

I had a knot in my stomach and didn't get anything more than scrambled eggs and orange juice. I didn't think I'd be able to eat even that. As I turned to follow my mom and dad to our table I saw Louis's parents. And seated there at the table with them was Louis.

I'M NOT SURE how long I stood there, just staring. Finally, somebody jostled me as they tried to pass with their tray, and I made my way over to where my parents were sitting. I watched him throughout the meal, and there was no doubt about it: Louis was alive.

I told my parents I changed my mind about going to shore and then rushed to find Tony. He didn't believe me and only went along with me to their cabin to shut me up. When we got to their corridor, they were just leaving the cabin. Louis was chatting and laughing. We followed them to the gangway leading to shore.

As they were preparing to leave the ship, Tony shouted, "Hey, Louis."

Louis looked over at us and frowned. He said something to his parents and then walked over to us.

"What's up?" Tony said, grinning as if they were old pals.

Louis looked from him to me and asked, "What do you want?"

"Hey," Tony said, "what do you mean? We're your friends, right? We were just wondering how you were doing."

"I'm doing fine," Louis answered and started to leave.

Tony grabbed his arm. "Come on, you've got to tell us," he begged. "What happened last night?"

"My *real* friends saved me," he answered and then rejoined his parents and left the ship.

I WOULD HAVE just let it drop there, but Tony had to know who these "real friends" were and what had really happened. Tony claimed he wanted to make sure we weren't going to get in trouble, but I knew that wasn't the real reason. Just like looking behind the CREW ONLY doors, he was simply dying of curiosity. I hinted that we should just forget about it, but he accused me of chickening out.

Louis and his parents didn't come back until dinner-time, carrying shopping bags and wearing straw hats. We followed them to their cabin and waited down the hall. About half an hour later, all three of them left for dinner. Tony and I tried to form a plan to get Louis alone but nothing worked. After dinner, they went back to their cabin, but Louis's parents left again almost immediately. This was our chance.

Tony wanted to knock on the door, but I didn't think Louis would open it for us. We were arguing back and forth about what we should do when the cabin door opened and Louis emerged carrying a suitcase.

"Where are you going with the suitcase?" Tony asked.

"Nowhere," Louis said, not looking at either of us.

"Who are these 'real friends' of yours?" I tried.

Louis snorted. "Yeah, like I'd tell you."

"Oh, you'll tell us all right," Tony said. He grabbed Louis's suitcase and headed up the stairs. Louis glared at him but followed us up to the deck. The sun had just set. The ship had left port during dinner and the nearby islands were outlined in lights as we glided across the ocean. Tony dangled the suitcase over the rail.

"Tell us what happened last night," he said, "or I'll pants you."

Louis didn't cry or get mad or anything. Instead, he kind of half smiled. I was impressed, a little guy like him not scared.

"Fine," he replied. "but first I want you to apologize for nearly getting me killed last night. Both of you."

Tony and I each mumbled, "I'm sorry," and then Louis told us his story.

"As I was falling last night, a beam of light hit me. I fell more and more slowly, and then the beam started to lift me up. I rose up into this space ship that I couldn't even see from the outside, and there were aliens on board. They were only supposed to watch us, but they couldn't let me die. They asked me if I wanted to go with them to learn about other worlds."

"And you said no," Tony jeered, but he didn't seem as confident as usual.

"I said yes," Louis told him. "But I asked for one more day to spend with my mom and dad before I left. That's why I packed my suitcase. I'm supposed to meet them at the same place I fell from last night."

Tony slowly pulled the suitcase back over the rail and handed it to Louis.

"You don't really believe that, do you?" I asked Tony.

He glared at me. "What if I do? Don't you believe in aliens? Besides, what other reason can you think of besides aliens?"

He had me there. I couldn't explain it. I still didn't buy Louis's alien story, but I didn't want to argue with Tony. Louis took his suitcase and left. Tony was practically bouncing around with excitement.

"We have to go check this out," he said, "but first we have to go get my camera. Can you believe it? *Real aliens!* And if we get pictures, we'll be famous."

As we went to get his camera, Tony talked on and on about what the aliens might look like and how long they had been here and where they were from. I thought he was crazy, but I didn't say anything. I had a bad feeling about the whole thing, but no way was I going to back down. What could happen?

When we reached the spot by the rail, we found Louis sitting on his suitcase, looking up at the stars. He didn't seem surprised or upset to see us. I pulled over a nearby deck chair while Tony fussed with his camera.

We waited nearly an hour. Tony occasionally asked questions about the aliens, but Louis's only reply was "You'll see."

Finally Louis stood and walked to the rail. He raised himself up on his tiptoes to get a good look over it. After a few seconds he said, "My ride is here."

Tony rushed to his side, holding his camera ready. I hadn't heard anything, but a knot of fear was twisting in my gut. Still, I couldn't stand back and do nothing, or

Tony would think I was scared. I stepped forward to the rail and stood at Louis's other side.

We looked down into the darkness and listened to the rush and roar of the water below.

"I don't see anything," Tony said anxiously.

"No," Louis agreed, "but trust me, they're down there."

Then he reached out and grabbed me by the wrist. His other hand grabbed Tony's.

"However," Louis said, smiling now, "you were right, Brad. They're not aliens."

I tried to pull my wrist free, but Louis's grip seemed to have superhuman strength.

"They came for me after I fell," Louis said. "They came in black robes and pulled me from the dark water. They told me my time in the land of the living was up, but I begged for one more day. Just one more day. You know why?"

I tried to drag myself away from the rail, but Louis was anchored like a statue.

"Because if I had to go, I didn't want to go *by myself.*"

He climbed up onto the rail, easily pulling me and Tony up with him.

"No, please," I begged as we stood balanced there, the darkness rushing below.

Louis turned his head and smiled at me.

"What's the matter?" he said, just before stepping off the rail. "You aren't chicken, are you?"

NATURE'S REVENGE

Jackie followed her father along the short path to Big Will's Trading Post. The store was set up high on stilts, so they had to climb a steep bamboo staircase to enter. The place was just the way Jackie remembered it, with bunches of bananas hanging from the rafters, open casks of nails, blankets piled in a corner, canned food stacked on open shelves, and a rack of colorful tropical print shirts, just like the ones Big Will himself always wore.

"Jackie!" Big Will called from behind the grill where several hamburger patties sizzled. He wore an apron over a loud Hawaiian shirt. Except for a few extra pounds and more gray in his crewcut, Big Will looked just the same. "Pull up a seat. I've got your favorite coming up," Big Will said. "Flash, how you doing?"

Her father waved at the mention of his nickname. All his friends called him Flash because he was always taking pictures. After the navy, he became a professional photographer. It was pretty exciting, Jackie thought. He spent the year sailing around the world and taking pictures for books and magazines. Jackie's parents divorced when she was seven, and she had spent the five summers since then sailing all over the world with her dad on his photography assignments. It had been two years since their last visit to this island in the Philippines, so she was surprised and pleased that Big Will remembered her.

Jackie climbed up on a stool by the lunch counter. Her father went over to check in with the regulars, a group of jungle guides and sailors watching a baseball game on a small black-and-white television. A chorus of "Flash!" rose, and Jackie smiled. Her father had friends in every port, it seemed.

Big Will scooped chocolate ice cream into a sundae dish and then topped it off with pineapple and whipped cream.

"There you go," he said as he handed Jackie her favorite dessert.

"I can't believe you remembered," Jackie gasped, snatching up the spoon.

"We call it the Jackie Special now. It's very popular." He leaned his heavy frame on the counter across from her. "So how's the picture taking going this summer?"

Jackie couldn't stop herself from wrinkling her forehead and frowning.

"That bad, huh?"

"Dad got this book contract to take photos of wrecked ships and planes from World War II. But he's under a tight deadline, so we've been sailing all over the place," Jackie explained. "The summer's more than half over, and it seems like I've hardly gotten to spend any time with him. All he does is work."

"That's rough," Big Will said. "Have you talked to him about it?"

Jackie brightened as she remembered the conversation. "Yeah, we did last night. We came to the Philippines to get photos of some wreck off Koljitua Island, but he said we can spend a couple of days in Manila first. We're going to be tourists, and he promised not to do any work. I can't wait."

"Sounds like fun," Big Will agreed, then asked. "You going to dive when you get to Koljitua Island?"

"Of course," Jackie said. "I always carry dad's camera bag for him."

"Well, keep your eyes open. No telling what you'll find."

"What do you mean?" Jackie inquired.

"They call Koljitua the Atlantis of the South Pacific," Big Will told her. "They say while the natives on the other islands were fighting with spears and living in huts, the people of Koljitua built a huge city with running water and statues on every corner."

"So what happened to it?" Jackie asked.

"The island's a volcano, and the people harnessed its power for their city. But many people believe that by doing this they angered the volcano gods, and the gods made the volcano erupt. *Koljitua* means 'nature's revenge.' It wiped the city off the face of the earth, but divers occasionally find traces offshore—coins, ceramic pieces, stuff like that. So keep your eyes open."

"I will," Jackie promised. "But even if I find a whole chest full of treasure, it's not going to be as cool as spending time with Dad in Manila."

Her father joined them at the counter. "Hey, Will," he said. "I've got a list of the supplies we need."

Will took the list and nodded as he read over it.

"We need it fast too," Jackie's father added. "We've got to get going, pronto."

Jackie stopped eating and looked at her father. "What's the hurry? It's only a few hours to Manila."

"Change of plans." He nodded at the men watching TV. "The boys say bad weather's moving in. If we don't head for Koljitua today, we won't be able to get our shots there for a week, and I'll miss my deadline."

"What about Manila?" Jackie asked, tears forming in the corners of her eyes.

"Sorry, sweetheart. There's no room in the schedule for our side trip now. Maybe we'll have some spare time to play tourist when we get to Hawaii next month. How does that sound?"

Jackie looked down at her sundae. "Sure, Flash," she whispered. She couldn't bring herself to call him Dad. He hardly seemed like her father any longer.

WHEN THEY REACHED Koljitua Island late that afternoon, Jackie's father lowered the sails and dropped anchor. Jackie sat on the foredeck and studied the island. It rose up in a cone shape, with a jagged crater at the top. Lush jungle vegetation covered the slopes up to the very rim. From the size of some of the trees, she knew the volcano had not erupted in a very, very long time.

Jackie's father busied himself unpacking scuba gear from the deck lockers. Jackie stayed where she was.

"Come on, kiddo," he finally said. "Time to get suited up."

He held up her pink-and-purple wet suit, but she didn't move.

"Are you ready to go?" he asked.

After a few moments of silence, she answered, "No. I'm not going down."

He frowned. While part of her felt horrible for saying no to him, she was determined to stick to her decision.

"Why not? Come on, we're a team," he implored.

"We're not a team," she said. "I just carry your camera bag sometimes. You get along fine without me nine months of the year. You won't even notice I'm not there."

"Of course I will," he said, putting down the wet suit. "Are you still angry that I canceled our trip to Manila? Because—"

"No, Flash!" she interrupted him. "I'm mad about spending this whole terrible summer by myself."

"We've spent all summer together," he protested. "We can spend time diving together now."

"We can't even talk to each other when we're diving— which is pretty much what the rest of the summer has been like."

"That's not true," he said.

"Could have fooled me."

He stood there for a minute and then finally sighed heavily. "Well, I have to go down and get pictures of this PT boat. If you don't want to go, that's fine. We'll talk about this more when I get back."

Neither of them spoke as he geared up. She kept her back to him, but she could feel him looking at her and waiting for her to say something. Then came the splash as he dropped into the water. Jackie finally let out the tears she'd been holding in. Sobs shook her for a minute and she whispered, "I have no father."

JACKIE WENT BELOW to wash her face. She didn't want her father to know she had been crying. Then she started to pack her things. The next time they came to an island with an airport she was going to fly home. She didn't care if she weren't due home for another month. She couldn't stand to spend any more time being ignored by her own father.

She started to pack. After filling her duffel bag with all her clothes, toiletries, and souvenirs, she grabbed her alarm clock. Looking down at the second hand moving around the dial, she was gripped with panic. Her father had been underwater for a very long time.

Jackie hadn't checked her watch when he dove as she usually did. Flash's tank held an hour's worth of air, but as a safety precaution he never stayed down more than 40 minutes. How long had it been? It felt like at least 40 minutes. Maybe longer.

Jackie dashed to the side of the boat where he had dived but saw nothing, no bubbles, no trace of him. Scuba diving could be very dangerous, even when you were completely focused. But she had started an argument with him before he dove. He was upset and distracted. Jackie pictured him trapped or injured at the bottom of the ocean and felt sick with guilt.

She quickly pulled on her wet suit and wasted no time putting together the rest of her diving equipment: mask, weight belt, vest, air tank, fins. With her regulator and air hose clamped between her teeth, she tumbled backward into the water.

The wreck—a patrol torpedo boat about the same size as their sailboat—rested about 30 feet down. Jackie swam toward it, searching for any sign of her father. A manhole-size gash in the steel hull was obviously the cause of the boat's sinking. Jackie headed toward it, imagining her father trapped inside, his air running out. When she reached the hole she could see nothing in the darkness within. In her rush she had forgotten to bring a flashlight. But her father had one in his camera bag, and if he was in there, he would be using it to signal her now, she thought. Unless he were pinned under something or unconscious.

A shadow passed overhead, filling Jackie with dread. Without hesitation, she plunged through the hole into the black interior of the wreck. Looking back, she watched a 15-foot shark knifing silently through the water. She had been in the water with sharks before, and though she knew they probably wouldn't attack her unprovoked, they still terrified her.

Inside the wreck, her eyes slowly adjusted to the gloom. She was in a small compartment with no unobstructed passages leading out of it, so she knew her father had not come this way. Peering out of the wreck's hole, she saw no sign of the shark. But she was reluctant to leave the safety of the boat while it might still be lurking nearby. She knew she couldn't hide in here forever, with her father missing and her own air running out.

It was while she was scanning the shadows for some sign of the shark that she noticed the object. It looked smooth and rounded and seemed unnatural among the rough black rocks. A feeling of dread made it difficult to breathe when she recognized it. Without further thought of the shark, she shot out of the wreck and kicked her way to the object to get a closer look. Just as she had feared, she saw it was her father's air tank, lying discarded among the black sand and rock.

Jackie looked around wildly for some other sign of her father and caught sight of a mysterious opening a few yards away where the rock rose toward shore in a sheer black wall. The surface of the round opening had a weird, glistening appearance, making it look like a liquid mirror.

As Jackie swam closer, something gave her hope: Her father would have fit through the hole, but only if he had taken off his air tank. She reached out and touched the surface of the strange substance. It felt cool and slick. She forced her hand through and felt an odd resistance, as if trying to push through gelatin. She was scared but didn't feel she had much choice. Desperate to find her father, she kicked her flippers and squeezed through, barely fitting with her own air tank on.

On the other side of the opening, Jackie found herself still underwater and surrounded by craggy black stone. She kicked the short distance to the surface and found she was in a tide pool. She pulled off her mask to get a better look at her surroundings.

It took her a few minutes, but she finally recognized she was at the shores of the island of Koljitua. Across the black sand beach a multileveled city rose, climbing up the side of the volcano. The rim of the volcano's crater, she noticed, was no longer jagged. A frozen river of smooth black stone spilled from the rim all the way down through the city to the beach. The cold, hardened stone had destroyed all it had touched, though most of the city remained intact.

This was it, Jackie realized, the ancient civilization that Big Will had spoken of, the Atlantis of the South Pacific. Somehow the portal had taken her back in time, to Koljitua as it had been hundreds or thousands of years ago. She was so surprised and thrilled about traveling back in time that she almost forgot why she was there. She needed to find her father.

She climbed out of the pool and took off her fins, air tank, and weight belt. As she was setting them in the black sand, she saw the rest of her father's gear nearby and footprints leading away up the beach. So he really had come this way, she thought with relief.

Jackie walked barefoot through the sand. Her father's footprints led her to an avenue that wound up into the strange city. The buildings were all stone, with open doorways and windows. The stone had been painted white, though soot or smoke had caused it to turn gray over time. Jackie felt like a trespasser, but after looking in a few of the doors and windows she realized the city was empty of people. She followed the twists and turns of the avenue as it rose higher into the city.

The avenue led her to an open area where several streets met. At the center was a fountain spewing boiling water that smelled like rotten eggs. Jackie circled around it, staying as far away as possible.

She was deciding where to go next when she spotted her father farther up the avenue, taking pictures of a row of sculptures. She ran to him.

"Flash," she said quietly, afraid to speak more loudly in this strange place.

He spun around, a look of amazement on his face. "Isn't this unbelievable?"

She stepped closer as he continued to take pictures of the sculptures.

"These shots are going to make me famous, kiddo," he said as he worked. "*Nature, National Geographic, Scientific American*—they're going to be begging to publish these shots. The only recorded evidence of a lost civilization. No, it's bigger than that. We're talking *Time* and *Newsweek*, interviews, talk shows. We've discovered a way to travel back in time. We'll be famous!"

"But why was it lost?" Jackie asked. "Where is everybody?"

Her father shrugged. "Who knows?"

Jackie turned around to look back the way she had come. Beyond the winding street and rows of white stone buildings, beyond the black beach and across the glimmering blue sea, thousands of boats covered the water like a flock of seagulls. Jackie rummaged through her father's camera bag and pulled out a pair of waterproof binoculars. Peering through them, she saw the boats were filled to the rails with people. The boats were sailing away from the island, and the people on board were looking back expectantly.

"Flash," she said, "I think you—"

Before she could warn him, the ground beneath them started to tremble. She staggered as the ground rose and fell and shook, worse than the sailboat during a storm. A great roar came from the crater. Jackie looked up as a great spray of smoke and ash erupted from it, filling the sky. Over the rim oozed a mass of glowing red lava that flowed down the slope directly toward them in a solid wall higher than the city's tallest building.

"Run!" her father yelled as he spun toward her, snatching up his heavy camera bag by its strap.

They bolted back the way she had come. She heard the lava's burning roar as it hit the first of the city's white stone buildings and began filling the streets behind them. Jackie ran as fast as she could down the middle of the twisting street, but the quaking ground made it hard to keep her balance. As she swerved around the steaming fountain, her left foot bent inward. A tearing pain shot up her leg and she fell, scraping her hands on the rough stone of the fountain's basin.

Jackie knew she had no time to stop. She was trying to push herself up when her father reached her. She clutched at the strap on his camera bag to pull herself to her feet. The strap broke, and she and the heavy bag fell again.

The roar of rushing lava grew louder. Her father asked, "Can you make it?" He picked up the heavy camera bag the only way he could now, hugging it to his chest with both arms.

Jackie pushed herself up again. Though pain tore through her leg, she knew he could not help her and carry his camera gear. She nodded that she was okay and then took several hobbling steps, grimacing in pain.

Without a moment's hesitation, he dropped his camera bag and threw her over his shoulder. Looking behind, she watched as lava oozed toward the bag. The lava was gaining on them.

When they reached the open beach moments later, her dad headed toward the tide pool in an all-out sprint. Jackie looked up the slope of the mountain. Its upper reaches were buried and its lower streets glowed with fire. The lava emerged from the path behind them and at many other points up and down the beach, cutting them off from land. It was so close, Jackie had to shield her eyes from the heat.

Her father lowered her into the tide pool. Jackie snatched up her mask but had to abandon the rest of her gear. She plunged into the pool, groped her way to the hole in the bottom, and pulled herself through. As soon as she reached the other side the roaring and shaking was shut off. It was as if a heavy, soundproof door had slammed closed.

Jackie swam over to her father's discarded air tank. Her scraped palms stung from the salt water, but she ignored the pain as she turned the release and took a deep breath from the mouthpiece. Then she carried the tank over to her father, who had just emerged from the hole. She pushed the mouthpiece against his lips. His hands found it, and he took a deep breath before giving her another turn. Jackie hadn't practiced buddy breathing since her father first trained her how to dive years ago, but the lessons were paying off. During her father's next turn, she watched as the red-hot lava pushed through the hole like toothpaste. The water boiled and sizzled, and great clouds of steam rose toward the surface. When it cleared, the portal was sealed with cold black stone.

Jackie knew her father could not see clearly without a mask, so she started to lead him toward the spot where the sailboat was anchored. Buddy breathing made for slow progress, but they had plenty of air left and no reason to hurry. During her father's turn breathing, she grabbed his arm and kicked toward the boat, looking over her shoulder to get her bearings. Her heart felt as if it were going to explode when she saw the familiar gray form gliding along a dozen yards to her left. She glanced at her scraped palms, which looked as if they were covered with tiny rubies where she was bleeding. The shark, smelling the blood, would come right for her.

Jackie knew what she had to do. She yanked the air tank away from her father and let it sink to the bottom. Then she swam away from him, heading up. With no air, he would have to go directly to the surface. He was not the one bleeding. The shark would leave him alone to go after her—she hoped.

When she reached the surface, he was already there, 10 yards away.

"Shark!" she called. "Quick, get back to the boat!"

Her father started swimming with strong strokes. Taking a deep breath, Jackie dove back under. She scanned the water nearby for the shark as she headed toward the boat. She saw the shark a dozen yards away, heading for her father. Horrified, Jackie waved her bleeding hands. The shark twitched and changed directions, now pursuing her. She knew she would never make it to the boat in time to escape, so she went down instead, kicking madly even though her ankle throbbed with pain. With the shark easily gaining on her, Jackie felt her way to the sunken PT boat and pulled herself inside. The shark plunged after her but became wedged in the hole. Just inches from her face, the shark's jaws opened and closed like a machine, showing her rows of jagged teeth. Then it pulled itself free and swam out of sight.

Jackie's lungs were burning, and she was starting to feel lightheaded from lack of air. She did not have much time, certainly not enough to wait for the shark to leave. Looking straight up, she carefully removed her mask, holding it so that the air trapped inside did not escape. She exhaled the air she had been holding in her lungs and then positioned the mask over her mouth until she was able to breathe in that small amount of air. Then she dropped the mask, swam to the hole, and took hold of its edges. All she could see was the sailboat's blurry shadow against the brilliant surface above. She would not know if the shark were waiting for her until its teeth ripped into her. But she had no other choice.

She pulled herself out by the edges of the hole with both hands and then kicked off the hull, launching herself toward the surface. She kicked and stroked with all her remaining energy until she erupted out of the water like a dolphin. She glanced around quickly to get her bearings and saw that she had judged the distance well—the boat ladder was only 10 feet away. She swam to it, and then her father pulled her out of the water, up onto the sunny deck. He hugged her fiercely.

"I'm sorry," she said. "I'm so sorry."

He pulled away and looked at her, puzzled. "For what?"

"For making you lose all your cameras and all the pictures you took. If it wasn't for me, you'd be famous. You can't even go back and take more."

He laughed and hugged her again. "A choice between you and being famous isn't a choice at all. You'd win every time," he told her. "I'm the one who should be sorry. If I hadn't canceled our plans in Manila, none of this would have happened. I guess you were right. I haven't done much this summer to show you how much I appreciate having you with me. Will you let me make it up to you?"

Jackie was grinning and crying at the same time. "I don't know. You've got two months to make up for and only one month left."

He tousled her short damp hair. "Then I should get busy, shouldn't I? Oh, and one other thing."

"What's that?" she asked.

"Do you think you could start calling me Dad again? Lots of people call me Flash, but you're the only who ever calls me Dad."

Jackie nodded happily. "You bet—Dad."

THE LIGHTHOUSE

"Help!" Carol screamed, dropping her sleeping bag and running toward the cars. Of all the scouts, troop leaders, and chaperones, Shannon was the only one who went to investigate the sleeping bag. The other scouts stood frozen in the act of setting up their tents. They all watched uneasily as Carol fled screaming, "It's huge! It's a monster!"

Mrs. Jensen, the troop leader, intercepted Carol and led her back toward the camp. Mrs. Jensen looked a little frightened herself, but she sounded calm as she asked, "What is it, Carol? What's wrong?"

Carol half hid behind Mrs. Jensen as they neared the sleeping bag. "This *huge* mosquito is stuck on my sleeping bag. I mean it's *huge*! It must be some kind of mutant."

Mrs. Jensen laughed. "It's just a mosquito, Carol. The woods are full of them."

"That's just it," Carol insisted. "What if there are *others*? This one is almost big enough to take my sleeping bag. A swarm of them could carry us all off!"

Mrs. Jensen let out an exasperated sigh and shook her head as they reached the sleeping bag. "You've had too much of *The X-Files*. But I must say, that is an awfully big mosquito."

Shannon quietly inspected the insect. It was as big as a silver dollar but appeared frail. "It's not a mosquito," she said, brushing it gently off the sleeping bag. "It's a crane fly. They don't bite."

Carol shrank back as the ungainly insect flew into the thick Maine woods. The other girls, who had moved in closer to see what was going on, now laughed and returned to setting up their tents.

"Thank you, Shannon," Mrs. Jensen said, chuckling to herself, and then announced, "Hurry up, girls. The ranger will be here soon to take us on our hike."

Carol poked her sleeping bag with the toe of her sneaker, as if afraid an army of other creepy-looking insects were about to make an appearance. "How'd you know that?" she asked Shannon. "Read about it in one of your books?"

"Yeah, in this nature guide I brought along," Shannon said. While the other girls had been singing or chatting on the bus on the way from Portland, she had been reading her nature guides, studying the sorts of trees, animals, and rocks they were likely to find here in Maine's Pelican Island State Park. To Shannon, the world was a vast, fascinating place, and she wanted to know everything about it. She planned to be a scientist when she grew up, though she wasn't sure exactly what kind. At age 10, she had plenty of time to decide.

"There's nothing on this island that can hurt you," Shannon explained to Carol. "Well, except maybe poison ivy and poison oak, but I can show you what those look like."

"Okay," Carol said. "Hey, do you have a partner for the scavenger hunt yet?"

Shannon shook her head.

"Can we be partners then? You're going to win easy."

RANGER POLKMAN TURNED up a few minutes later, jumping out of the woods and so scaring Glenda Snow that the firewood she had been gathering flew in all directions. Laughing, Ranger Polkman introduced himself and then asked everyone to follow him. Shannon was at the head of the troop as they followed along a narrow trail. She wanted to learn everything she could about the ecology of Pelican Island, though Ranger Polkman seemed more interested in scaring everyone than teaching them.

"Make sure you stay close to your campfires tonight," he advised. "There's no telling what kind of creatures may be lurking in these woods."

"Sure there is," Shannon contradicted him. "Squirrels, raccoons, and possums. I don't think they'll bother us."

Shannon didn't usually speak up in this way, but she was mad at Ranger Polkman for trying to scare them

because they were a bunch of girls. She guessed he would be behaving differently if they were a group of boys.

Surprisingly, Ranger Polkman just grinned at her. "Oh, a skeptic," he said. "You don't believe in monsters, unexplained forces, things that go bump in the night?"

"No," Shannon said. "Not really."

"Is that so?" he said. "Well, how about ghosts?"

Before she had a chance to answer, they emerged from the woods into an open area. This end of the island was sandy and grassy, with no trees. A concrete sidewalk circled a small, empty parking lot and led to the foot of a lighthouse. Near its whitewashed base were a small house and a shed. Shannon rushed to read the plaques that related facts about the lighthouse.

"Modern navigational technology has made lighthouses obsolete," Ranger Polkman recited. Shannon guessed that he had given this lecture many times before. "But for nearly 200 years, the Pelican Island Lighthouse helped steer passing vessels away from the treacherous rocks."

He droned on about the size of the lighthouse, how it had been constructed, and its history, apparently without even listening to his own words. But then, eyes gleaming with mischief, he turned and looked directly at Shannon.

"The last keeper of the Pelican Island Lighthouse was a man named Cecil Arthur. He lived in this small house. They say that being a lighthouse keeper is one of the loneliest jobs in the world, with no one to talk to and the heavy responsibility of keeping the light burning. Cecil had two part-time assistants who lived on the mainland, but most of the time it was just Cecil and his daughter, Holly. People thought it was good for him to have his daughter with him. They thought it would help keep him sane. But they were wrong."

He glanced at Shannon again. She was a little disturbed by the dark direction the story seemed to be taking, but she crossed her arms and tried to look bored.

"On a day much like today, a terrible nor'easter blew in. You've all grown up in Maine, so I don't need to tell you how powerful those storms can be. But close your eyes and try to imagine what it was like—out here all alone except for the lighthouse's beacon as the winds shrieked and the rains howled. The storm came without warning, so the assistants never had time to get here from the mainland—there was no road in those days. So it was up to Cecil and Holly to make sure the light kept burning."

"Mainlanders," he continued, "peering out into the storm, saw the light go out for the last time late that night. When Cecil's assistants arrived the next morning, they found Cecil and Holly at the foot of the lighthouse, dead. According to the police investigation, the storm and the isolation had been too much for Cecil. He went berserk and smashed up the light and the windows high atop the lighthouse. Holly begged him to stop, but he was insane. He grabbed her and threw her from the top of the lighthouse. Then realizing what he had done, he threw himself off as well, to join his daughter in death.

"But I can see you're not convinced," he said, looking right at Shannon. "Sure, it's just a story—where's the proof? Well, young ladies, follow me, and I'll show you."

He led them halfway around the base of the lighthouse, then stopped at a dark blotch on the whitewashed concrete. It looked as if someone had spilled dark paint there a long time ago. It was worn but clearly visible.

"This is the spot where the bodies were found," the ranger whispered in a low voice, barely over a whisper. "The stain you see was left by Cecil's and Holly's blood. It's lasted more than 50 years since their deaths. This spot has been scoured, sandblasted, and painted over many times, but the stain always bleeds through, an indelible reminder of the tragedy that took place here."

The ranger gave Shannon a triumphant grin and then started to lead the girls to the entrance to take them up to the top of the lighthouse. Carol shivered.

"Do you really think that's their blood?" Carol asked.

Shannon shook her head. "No way. It never would have lasted this long. There must be some logical, scientific explanation. Maybe it's something in the ground here that seeps up through the concrete, or maybe it's somebody's idea of a joke. I can't say for sure what it is, but I can say for sure what it isn't, and that's the blood of ghosts."

BY THE TIME they got back to camp after the tour, the chaperones had a late lunch ready. The aroma of cooking hamburgers and hot dogs filled the air. Shannon had one of each and decided that what she had read was true. Food really did taste better in the great outdoors.

"It's time for the scavenger hunt," Mrs. Jensen announced after lunch.

Everyone would have two hours to gather as many items as possible on the list. Shannon rushed to get her copy. As she was scanning the items, Carol grabbed her arm and turned away any other would-be partners.

"Sorry," Carol told Susan and then Glenda and Valerie. "She's taken. Too bad."

Some of the items would be a snap, Shannon thought, like an oak leaf and a wild onion—she had seen lots of them on the hike. Other items, like a rock containing a fossilized plant or sea creature, would be much more difficult. But Shannon was determined to get them all.

She set off into the forest with Carol trailing behind. Stepping gingerly, Carol suddenly jerked her foot back. "A snake crawled across my foot!" Carol screeched.

"There are no snakes on this island," Shannon said distractedly. "Keep your eyes open for pine trees. We need a pinecone."

After an hour and a half, Shannon had found all but one of the items on the list. "Aren't we done yet? This bag is getting really heavy," Carol complained. Carol's participation in the scavenger hunt was limited to carrying the plastic bag full of plants, rocks, feathers, and other treasures.

"You can take it back to camp if you want," Shannon told her. "I only need to find one more item, and I don't need the bag for it."

Carol eagerly took her up on the offer and scampered down the trail back toward camp. Shannon took a different route. The only item she still needed was a fossil-containing rock.

It wasn't surprising that she'd been having no luck finding one, considering this was a public park. Any fossils you could spot on the well-traveled trails would have been picked up long ago. She'd go off the trail, then. She could win without the fossil, but she couldn't resist the challenge of being the only one who got everything on the list. Glancing at her watch, she saw she still had half an hour left.

She pushed her way through the thick forest under-growth and down a slope toward what looked like an old streambed. That, she figured, would be an ideal place to find rocks. And find them she did, though none with fossils. She ranged through the island's thickly wooded slopes, examining every rock she came across. Still no luck.

Squinting to check a rock, she noticed how dark it had gotten. A rising wind slashed through the treetops, and dark clouds blotted out the setting sun. A storm was coming.

The darkness had sneaked up on her, and now every-thing looked the same in all directions. She started uphill, trying to calm herself, figuring she would come upon a trail eventually, and then it would be easy to find her way back to camp.

But she couldn't find a trail. As the darkness settled, Shannon plunged blindly through the shadowy woods. The wind shook the trees so loudly she couldn't hear her own footsteps. If she kept walking in a straight line, she figured, eventually she would reach the ocean. But in the dark for-est, how could she be sure she was walking in a straight line?

Gripped with terror, she spotted something through the trees: a light, strong for a moment, then eclipsed by blowing branches, then strong again. It had to be the camp, she thought, relieved. Mrs. Jensen must have put out a lantern to guide the girls who still hadn't returned. Shannon hoped she wasn't the only one. That would be so embarrassing.

As Shannon trudged toward the light, the black clouds overhead broke open and rain fell in great, drenching sheets. Even in the forest, the cold, heavy drops found her. This was no simple storm. They were in for a full-fledged nor'easter.

Pulling herself free of the tangled branches and emerging from the woods, Shannon realized the light did not come from any lantern. It came from the abandoned lighthouse.

It didn't make sense—Ranger Polkman had said the lighthouse was no longer in use. But she made her way anyway toward it, trudging through sand and clumps of sawgrass, because it looked like a safe place to take shelter. A sudden bolt of lightning lanced out of the black sky and struck the lighthouse. Shannon watched in awe as the lightening connected the tall white tower to the sky for a moment, then disappeared. The light in the lighthouse also vanished. Thunder followed, and the air seemed to rumble along her skin.

When she reached the base of the dark lighthouse, she noticed someone hunched over, struggling in the rain. A girl around Shannon's age looked up. The hood of the girl's slicker had fallen back, and her hair hung in sopping brunet tangles.

"Get caught in the storm?" the girl asked. At her feet was an odd contraption made of thick, heavy glass with brass fittings. It resembled an old hurricane lamp that

Shannon's grandmother kept on the mantle but was much larger. The glass oil reservoir looked big enough to hold 20 gallons. "You can go in the house and warm up, if you want. The stove's lit. Or, if you're not too tired, you could give me a hand."

The girl struggled to lift the glass device but only managed to get it a few inches off the ground. She moved it several feet before having to set it down again with a heavy clunk.

"Sure, I'll help," Shannon said. She had an odd feeling about the whole situation, but she couldn't just stand by while the poor girl labored alone. She grabbed the oil lamp from the other side, and together they managed to carry it all the way into the lighthouse, right to the foot of the stairs.

"This is good," the girl said, breathing heavily from the effort. "Let's rest for a second before we start on the steps."

The cement stairs corkscrewed up into a darkness broken only by the light of a few oil lamps. "We have to carry this all the way to the top?" Shannon asked.

The girl nodded. "The lightning knocked out the electrical system. With a storm like this, we must keep the light burning to guide the ships out at sea. Many lives are at stake. All we have to use now is the old oil lamp. By the way, my name's Holly."

A chill shot through Shannon's body and she shivered. It was more than just the cold rain soaking her clothes. Holly was the name of the daughter of Cecil Arthur, the mad lighthouse keeper. "Do you believe in ghosts?"

Ranger Polkman had asked. Shannon was no longer sure. Holly reached out to shake hands.

"My name's Shannon," she said, reaching out to shake Holly's hand. Shannon half expected her fingers to slip through the hand as if it were mist, but it felt real enough.

"Okay," Holly said. "We can't waste any more time. Ready?"

They hefted the lamp and climbed slowly up the spiral staircase. Shannon noticed something very strange. A chain strung at waist level served as a railing, but earlier this afternoon she remembered leaning against a tubular steel railing. Mrs. Jensen had reprimanded one of the girls for sitting on it.

What did this mean? There had to be a reasonable explanation for all this, she reminded herself, one without ghosts. Could she have somehow traveled back in time 50 years? The thought almost made her laugh out loud. Too many science fiction books, she told herself. Time travel was about as likely as ghosts were.

But what else could explain the staircase rail and Holly? I know, she thought, I'm dreaming. I fell down in the woods, hit my head on a rock, and am lying in the dead leaves, dreaming this whole thing. But it didn't feel like a dream.

Then it hit her. I know exactly what is going on, she realized with a smile. She had only Ranger Polkman's version of the history of the lighthouse, and he had been trying to frighten her and the other girls. What if he had lied about the lighthouse no longer being in use? The girls, seeing the lighthouse lit up at night, would then get scared. And if the current keepers were named Holly and Cecil, and the girls ran into them, they would think the man and his daughter were ghosts!

That had to be it, Shannon thought, congratulating herself on using logic instead of panicking. But that still didn't explain the rail . . .

They reached the top, and despite Shannon's firm belief there was no such thing as ghosts or time travel, Shannon was seized by another shiver. Here at the top of the lighthouse, at the height of a storm just like this one, Cecil Arthur supposedly had gone insane and thrown his own daughter to her death.

The glass windows surrounding the little round chamber at the top let in powerful flashes of lightning. A short man wearing coveralls and round spectacles lay on the ground, surrounded by tools. He removed the electric light from the center of the room.

"Here it is, Dad," Holly announced as they put down the lamp. "My new friend, Shannon, helped me carry it up."

He gave her a shy, friendly grin. "We need all the friends we can get at the moment," he said. "Glad to know you, Shannon. My name's Cecil Arthur, by the way."

"Come on," Holly told her. "Now we have to go back down and get the oil."

As they hurried back down the steps, Shannon realized how ridiculous her fears about Cecil seemed now. That kind man an insane killer? If she weren't so cold, wet, and tired she probably would've found the whole situation hilarious.

IT TOOK FOUR trips up and down the twisting staircase to carry the heavy cans of oil to the top of the lighthouse. By the time they had brought up the fourth and last load of oil, Cecil had moved the electric light out of the way and stationed the oil lamp on the rotating platform at the center of the small room.

Frequent flashes of lightning outside the huge glass windows of the chamber briefly lit up the wind-lashed sea. The waves were whipping up the beach, almost to the base of the tower. After several hours, the storm wasn't dying down, it was growing stronger. The rain pelted the thick glass windows hard enough to rattle the panes.

"Now we're all set except for one last thing," Cecil said as he finished reassembling the replacement lamp, its reservoir now filled with oil. He fished out a metal cigarette lighter from his coveralls and lit the lamp. The tiny room was soon filled with a rich golden light. He positioned a round mirror on the lamp and then started the mechanical platform. As the platform turned, a bright beam of light sprang into the darkness, slicing through the night.

But just as they were starting to relax, the storm, as if dared by their efforts, increased its fury. The lighthouse was sturdy, with two-foot-thick walls of cemented stone, yet Shannon had to steady herself against its battering by the winds outside. The sheets of rain turned to hail. Golf ball-size pellets attacked the lighthouse, like machine gun bullets. The large windows facing the sea began to crack and then gave way entirely, shattering in pieces that scattered around the room. Shannon shielded her face with her arms to protect herself against the flying glass. The wind swept into the room and snuffed out the light.

Shannon braced herself against the wall, afraid the wind was going to carry her out into the storm. She watched as Holly's and Cecil's silhouettes picked their way carefully through the broken glass and pellets of hail that littered the floor. Cecil came toward her.

"Try to keep the lamp lit," he shouted over the roar of the storm, pressing his lighter into her hand.

Shannon nodded and felt silly, realizing he couldn't see the gesture in the darkness. She stepped carefully to the lamp and found it no longer rotating. She pulled off the glass hood and flicked the lighter, but even keeping the lighter lit was nearly impossible with the fierce winds whipping through the room.

The pounding hail stopped. Cecil pulled out six panes of glass to replace the broken ones in the windows facing the sea. He and Holly had to climb out on the narrow iron walkway that circled the outside of the lighthouse. As she tried to relight the lamp, Shannon could see them out of the corner of her eye, struggling as they carried one of the replacement panes out onto the catwalk. The sheet of glass caught the wind like a sail, and they wobbled as they tried to maintain their balance.

As if by one of the bolts of lightning hitting the lighthouse, Shannon was struck by a realization. She now knew what had really happened 50 years ago. Cecil had not gone insane and smashed up the lighthouse—the hail had done its damage and then melted by the time investigators arrived the next day. And, she realized with a rush of fear, Cecil had not thrown himself or Holly from the top of the lighthouse. They had fallen.

Shannon rushed toward them as Holly, unable to hold the large pane of glass in the strong wind, fell over the edge of the walkway. Cecil dropped the glass he was holding and lunged to grab her. Then he, too, vanished over the edge. Shannon clambered out the window and onto the catwalk where she could see Cecil's white-knuckled hand barely clinging to the rail. His other hand gripped Holly by the wrist. Holly's screams pierced the storm as the wind swung her from side to side and her legs kicked above 80 feet of empty air.

Shannon jumped into action. She threw herself flat on the walkway and wrapped her legs around one of the iron bars supporting the rail. Once she was braced, she reached down and was able to grab Holly's wrist with both hands. With Cecil's help, she managed to haul up his daughter until Holly could grab one of the iron supports and pull herself back onto the walkway. Then she and Shannon both helped Cecil get back up.

Cecil berated himself for being so careless and then used a rope to rig up safety lines. When he'd finished, he and Holly focused on replacing the panes of glass while Shannon returned to the lamp. She managed to get it lit. It blew out every few minutes over the hour it took to replace all the windows, but Shannon stood ready to relight it each time. With the last pane replaced, the lamp burned steadily.

Shannon slowly lowered herself to the floor with Cecil and Holly, all exhausted from their efforts.

"We have to thank you for your help out there," Cecil said. "Thanks to you, maybe this time we'll get to see the morning light . . . and whatever comes next."

Shannon was so tired, she could barely stay awake, but something about what he had said sounded odd. "'This time?'" she said. "What do you mean?"

"The storm has come every night for a very long time," Holly said, her voice a mix of sadness and hope. "This is the first time it's ever ended differently. Maybe . . ."

But sleep claimed Shannon before Holly finished her thought.

SHANNON WOKE TO the sound of her name being called. Her muscles ached from carrying the lamp and oil up the stairs the night before. She was surprised to find herself at the base of the lighthouse, by the padlocked door. Mrs. Jensen, some of the scouts, and several rangers were rushing across the parking lot toward her. Other scouts and chaperones were emerging from the woods. The morning sun had barely climbed above the horizon.

"Shannon!" Mrs. Jensen said as she reached her. "We were worried to death about you. Are you all right?"

"Yeah, I'm fine," Shannon said, trying to get her bearings. That padlock hadn't been on the lighthouse last night, nor had any of the plaques. And how had she gotten down here? She remembered falling asleep at the top of the lighthouse. But was any of that real? It had felt real at the time, but now she wondered if it were a dream.

"Where have you been?" Ranger Polkman asked. He was unshaven and seemed more serious than yesterday.

"Right here," Shannon said, deciding to say nothing about Cecil and Holly. No one would ever believe her anyway. "I came here to get out of the storm."

"What storm?" Mrs. Jensen asked.

Shannon glanced around. There should have been puddles everywhere, but the area was dry. Pamphlets and brochures that should have been blown halfway to Brazil were still in their plastic holders.

"Um, sorry," she said. "I guess I was just dreaming about a storm. I got lost in the woods during the scavenger hunt, and by the time I found the lighthouse, I was too tired to make it back to camp."

They all seemed satisfied with her explanation, and Shannon wondered if maybe it weren't the truth. Mrs. Jensen was wrapping her in a blanket when Glenda yelled out, "Hey, look! It's gone!"

Shannon joined those running around the base of the lighthouse to see what the shouting was all about. Glenda was pointing at the spot on the concrete where Ranger Polkman had shown them the unexplainable stain. It was gone. Ranger Polkman seemed flabbergasted and looked around as if the stain might have moved.

Mrs. Jensen and the other chaperones gathered every-one together and started marching them back toward camp for breakfast. Shannon followed behind, lost in thought. She remembered what Holly had been saying as

Shannon fell asleep. After 50 years, the storm had ended differently, and Holly and Cecil's long night was over.

Carol was waiting by the side of the trail to join Shannon. "Hey, partner, in case you were wondering, we won the scavenger hunt!" she said.

Still thinking about Cecil and Holly, Shannon failed to reply.

"Well, I guess you were right," Carol said after a moment.

Curious, Shannon looked over at her. "About what?"

Carol waved at the lighthouse behind them. "The stain. There wasn't anything special about it after all, just like you said."

Shannon put her hands in her pockets and felt the cold metal of Cecil's lighter under her fingertips.

"Don't listen to me," she said. "I don't know everything."

THE MERMAID'S KISS

Toby hated being a kid. Kids weren't allowed to do anything. Grownups never took him seriously. Well, he wanted to be an architect and wasn't going to wait until he grew up to start. He already had begun preparing and studying. He read books on architecture, he drew floor plans, and he kept files on famous buildings he wanted to visit someday.

When his parents told him he could choose where they'd go for their summer vacation, he picked Greece, the birthplace of classical architecture. They wanted to go somewhere "more fun" and tried to talk him into choosing a theme park in Florida or California, but his mind was made up. In the end they lied to him. Instead of taking him to Athens, they rented a villa on the beach of a small resort island. They were always trying to force him to be a kid, even if it meant he had to be miserable.

"What's wrong?" his mother asked after they arrived.

"I wanted to go to Greece and see the Parthenon and the other ancient ruins of the Acropolis," Toby said. "This place sucks."

"But we'll have fun," his dad said. "They've got a video arcade and a miniature golf course here."

"That stuff's for kids," Toby grumbled.

"You are a kid," his mom reminded him.

"That's not my fault."

They forced him to play Frisbee on the beach, board games in their rented villa, and miniature golf in town. But he didn't enjoy himself. Those childish games were pointless. Finally his parents gave up and left him alone. He spent most of his time inside, reading books and making drawings.

A couple of days after they arrived, Toby walked down to the beach and found his parents making a sand castle. They were using a plastic shovel and a stick as their tools, and their castle looked as if it had been hit by a tidal wave. Obviously they knew nothing about structural design.

Toby returned to the villa and came back with a collection of tin cans in assorted sizes, an ice chest, a water pitcher, and other kitchen utensils. He would show them how to make a *real* sand castle.

He packed sand in the ice chest, turned the chest upside down, and then carefully removed it. He packed sand in the tin cans to form turrets almost as tall as himself. Then he went to work shaping buttresses, ramparts, and square-toothed crenellations around the upper edge.

Toby didn't notice when his parents left. He didn't notice anything until his mother came to get him for dinner, and only then he realized it was getting dark.

HIS PARENTS WERE happy that he seemed to be enjoying himself. But they didn't understand what the sand castle meant to him. Building with the sand was a chance to finally *do* something with all he had learned from his architecture books. Instead of just reading and planning and dreaming, he was actually *creating* something.

So despite the stupid grins his parents gave him the next morning, Toby rushed to the beach where his sand castle still stood. He had come up with a grand plan. He would build an entire sand city.

He spent the morning using string and sticks to lay out roads. He rolled his city's streets flat with a tin can and curbed them with gravel from the driveway. He worked the rest of the day on the buildings, filling the block next to the castle with a Greek-style temple in the center of a park.

Soon he was spending his entire day constructing his city. He ransacked his parents' suitcases and the villa for objects to liven up his buildings: bits of costume jewelry for colorful widows and decorations, knickknacks to stand in as statues and monuments, and a round pocket mirror that simulated a reflecting pool.

One morning he was surprised to find that someone had added a walled garden with seashell paths, coral trees, and even a small pool in which a tiny sea anemone waved its crimson tentacles.

Toby looked up and down the beach for his uninvited assistant, but the beach was empty. He did find a set of footprints in the sand, but they ended at the water. Whoever added the beautiful garden must have walked along the surf to hide his or her footprints.

The next morning Toby rushed to the beach and found a new tower next to the garden. It had seven sides and twelve stories and was like no building he had ever seen in any of his architecture books. He studied it from every angle. He was amazed by the intricate detail of the structure, which included balconies with little polished white rails made from fish bones.

Toby worked on the city all morning, but his thoughts were on the mysterious person who was contributing to his city at night. The design of the tower was unique. Were there really buildings like that in the world? He doubted it, or he would have discovered them by now in his books. He was determined to find the answer.

That night Toby sneaked out his bedroom window and down to his sand city. The beach was empty so he decided to work while he waited for his unknown partner. By the light of the stars he sculpted a diamond-shaped building. He became so engrossed in what he was doing that he forgot why he was there. A sudden gasp behind him brought him out of his reverie.

He turned to see a girl running toward the ocean. Her dark wet hair stuck to her shoulders. Toby thought she looked younger than he was.

"Wait!" he called, but she either didn't hear or ignored him. She plunged into the ocean. Toby ran to the shore and continued calling to her. He stared at the ocean for what seemed like hours but, strangely, saw no sign of her.

THE NEXT MORNING Toby found the diamond-shaped building finished, with intricate designs of dried seaweed adorning its walls. The young girl must have returned after Toby had gone to bed. She must be shy, he thought, or afraid he would be mad at her, and this made him more determined to meet her. He wondered how he could have missed her coming up for air when she ran into the water.

He spent the afternoon digging a shallow pit several feet long, which he then built an arena around. It featured round windows along the upper edge, which he made by burrowing paper towel tubes through the sand.

That night he told his parents he was tired and going to bed early. Then he sneaked out the window and down the beach to the sand city. He carefully made his way to the oblong arena he had built and stepped inside its wall. He lay down in the shallow pit, making himself invisible to anyone on the beach. The cardboard tube windows he'd installed made perfect spy holes. He settled in for his surveillance of the beach.

AFTER A COUPLE of hours, in the light of the rising moon, Toby saw an amazing sight.

Another girl with long dark hair emerged from the water. She looked several years older than the girl from the night before. And she seemed to have trouble walking. Then he saw her tail, twice as long as her legs should have been. It glimmered and glistened blue in the moonlight. She slithered from the water onto the beach, but once she was clear of the surf, her tail transformed into a pair of slender legs.

Toby's jaw dropped. He couldn't believe it—a real mermaid!

She walked up the beach, carrying shells, driftwood, and bits of coral. He must have been mistaken about the girl from last night, he thought, as this was clearly the person who had been helping construct his city.

He waited nervously until she was only a few feet away, and then he stood. "Hi," he said uncertainly.

The mermaid screamed and dropped her building supplies. As she took a panicked step back toward the ocean, Toby called, "No, wait! I didn't mean to scare you. I'm sorry."

She paused and studied him, then smiled. "This is your city," she said.

"Well, technically I guess it's *our* city, since you've been adding to it too," Toby corrected her. "You're, um, pretty good."

She took a step closer. "My name is Lyriel."

"I'm Toby." He wasn't sure whether or not to shake hands, but the awkward moment passed as she knelt down to pick up what she had dropped.

"It looks like you have big plans for tonight," Toby observed as he helped her gather up the objects.

"Yes," she said. "I had planned to make a copy of the palace where my family lives. It's as tall as the Tower of Eternity, but even broader."

Toby glanced where she pointed, at the tower that had appeared yesterday morning.

"You mean that place really exists?" he asked. Imagining the building life-size filled him with awe.

"Oh, yes," she assured him. "There are many magnificent buildings in our city, as well as parks and gardens. The garden there is a replica of the one that surrounds the Pool of Lost Memories."

"Wow," Toby said. "I would give anything to see that."

Lyriel arched an eyebrow as she looked at him. "You would? There is a way, you know."

Toby felt his heart beat faster with excitement but also with fear. "Really?" he gasped.

Lyriel laughed. "Yes," she said. "But you mustn't stay long in the City of Ages, or your world will never be the same for you."

He figured the skyscrapers of his own world might seem boring after seeing the Tower of Eternity, but that was a chance he was willing to take. After all, he could design his own buildings after those of the seapeople. He would be the most famous architect of all time.

"Okay," he said. "Let's go."

She took his hand and led him down to the water. As it reached his waist, he started to worry.

"You do know I can't breathe underwater, don't you?" he said.

She laughed and then surprised him by kissing him.

"Wha—?" he started to ask when it was over, but before he could get the words out, she was diving beneath the sea, her long blue tail glistening like sapphires. She held his hand and pulled him beneath the surface.

He held his breath as long as he could stand and then exhaled. He started to panic, until suddenly he realized he was breathing underwater effortlessly.

"I don't understand," he said. "How am I breathing?"

Lyriel grinned over her shoulder at him as she pulled him deeper beneath the sea. "That's the magic of the mermaid's kiss."

Even towing Toby, Lyriel swam as swiftly as any fish. The water felt like a cool wind rushing past him. Lyriel carried him to a stony tunnel where mossy plants glowed on the walls with a soft green light. The cavern began to widen and deposited them on a slope above the magnificent City of Ages. The light from the buildings made the city seem as bright as day. Arches and bridges laced together delicate towers and paved streets glimmered like moonlight.

"Wow," he whispered as they floated above the city, his voice failing him in his amazement.

"What do you want to see first?" Lyriel asked.

"Everything," he told her.

THEY ENTERED THE city by following a grand boulevard made of stone blocks that gleamed a soft pink. Along with the ability to breathe and speak underwater, Lyriel's kiss allowed him to swim quickly and gracefully.

"Hey!" Toby shouted as he glided along. "I feel like Superman!"

Lyriel led him on an awe-inspiring architectural tour, starting with the garden surrounding the Pool of Lost Memories and the Tower of Eternity. The tower in particular thrilled him. He drifted through strange five-sided archways into different floors of the building. Lyriel explained that the tower was like a museum.

"Each level represents a different period in our history," she said.

Narrow rooms, radiating out from the center like the arms of a starfish, contained statues, paintings, and mosaics created with thousands of shells. But Toby was less interested in the building's contents than in the building itself. He drifted through arched entrances and strangely shaped rooms, admiring their design and committing it to memory. Someday he would recreate this building on land, and it was going to make him famous.

As they exited the Tower of Eternity, Lyriel told him, "You must leave the City of Ages now."

"Go back to the surface?" Toby asked. "Absolutely not. I've barely seen any of the city. Just the garden and this one tower."

"But I told you to not stay long. Your parents—"

"It's my decision," Toby said, tired of being treated like a kid, "not theirs. This is the chance of a lifetime, and I don't want to waste it. There's so much more to see." More buildings that he could study, to copy later when he became a working architect. The City of Ages was a treasure trove of ideas he could steal, with no one ever knowing.

"Very well," Lyriel agreed. "As you said, it's your decision. You're the one who must live with the consequences."

"Sure," Toby said. "So where should we go next?"

AFTER EXPLORING THE Tower of Eternity, Lyriel took him to the coral palace where her family had lived for thousands of years.

"This is awesome!" Toby exclaimed as he swam through the great hall, with its seven levels and dozens of passages leading to the rest of the place. "How many people live here?"

"Now?" Lyriel said. "Just me."

"But where are your parents? Oh, they're not, uh, dead, are they?"

"No," she explained. "Grown-up seapeople travel a lot. This isn't our only city."

"I hadn't thought of that. So how long have they been gone?"

Lyriel shrugged. "Have you seen any clocks or calendars? We age differently than you humans do. Time is less important to us."

Toby wanted to ask her a few more questions on the subject but was distracted by the spiral columns supporting the great hall's vaulted ceiling. He swam over for a closer look.

TOBY SLEPT ON a bed of bubbles, in a room with views of some of the city's most magnificent towers. Soon after he awoke, he and Lyriel dined in the great hall on shellfish and on sweet fruits that grew deep under the sea. But for Toby, sleeping and eating were simply chores to get out of the way so he could focus on exploring the City of Ages.

Lyriel showed him a sponge castle that was not just a building but a living thing. On another trip they visited an amphitheater with a great scallop-shaped roof supported by thousands of pencil-thin columns. They also toured a mighty fortress above a vast plain where Lyriel said many great battles had been fought, but which now was covered with hundreds of monuments.

Time started to lose meaning for Toby, as there was no day or night in the City of Ages. When he was hungry, he ate. When he was tired, he slept. The rest of the time, he studied and explored, cataloguing every detail in his mind.

The seventh time he awoke in his bed of bubbles, he felt sad and lonely. He missed his world. He missed his parents, even though they did treat him like a kid. He missed hamburgers and french fries, and he missed sleeping in a bed with blankets instead of bubbles.

He did not know how long he had been in the City of Ages, but he guessed about a week. Toby decided that he had accomplished all he could and was ready to return to his world.

He found Lyriel in the great hall and told her of his decision.

"Are you sure?" she asked. "As I told you before, your world will no longer be the same for you. If you're bored with this city, there are others we could go to."

"No. It's nice here, but I miss my home. Maybe I could come back again some time," Toby suggested.

Lyriel shook her head sadly. "I'm sorry. Once you return to the surface, you will never be able to visit here again."

Toby wasn't disappointed because he had already gathered enough knowledge about the city to last his whole career as an architect.

"That's okay," he said. "I still want to go back."

As Lyriel led him back through the City of Ages, Toby focused on taking one last look at the buildings around him to fix them in his memory.

At the cavern Lyriel took his hand and pulled him along. The glowing green moss passed in a blur, and then all was darkness. Suddenly he broke through the surface. Stars flashed overhead as he coughed and gasped. He let himself go limp as the waves pushed him toward shore. When his fingertips touched sand he dragged himself out of the water and up onto the beach.

Toby felt odd and off balance as he staggered up the sand. His arms and legs didn't seem to move correctly, and he mistakenly blundered into the middle of his sand city. He tried to catch himself, to keep from ruining all his hard work, but then he saw it was already ruined, trampled by countless footsteps.

"Who's there?" called a brusque voice, and then the beam of a flashlight stabbed through the darkness.

"Toby," he said. His voice sounded strange to him, coarser and deeper. "My name is Toby Wells. My family is staying in that villa."

As the person with the flashlight drew closer, Toby could see he was a police officer.

"Well, well," the officer said. "You must be the one we've been looking for. I thought you might come back here."

Of course, Toby thought. His parents would have called the police.

"I'm sorry," he said. "Have I been away long?"

"Away? You'll be going away for a very long time," the police officer said. He drew his gun and pointed it at Toby. "But it will be easier for you if you tell me what you did with Toby Wells."

"But . . . but I am Toby Wells."

The police officer only stared at him, waiting. With growing horror, Toby dug around in the sand with his fingers. The police officer watched him warily, until Toby finally found what he was looking for—the round mirror that had served as a reflecting pool. He looked at the face in it.

It was not his face. The face in the mirror was wrinkled, with only wisps of gray hair left. Trembling, Toby reached up to touch his face and saw the tangle of veins and wrinkles on the loose flesh of his hand. It was the hand of an old man.

"No!" Toby cried. "My parents . . ."

"Mr. and Mrs. Wells have gone back to America," the police officer said. "What did you do with their son?"

Slowly it all became clear. The young girl he had seen that first night, the one who had run away, had been Lyriel. That was why she looked older the second night.

"We age differently than you humans do." Lyriel's words came back to him. "You mustn't stay long in the City of Ages. Your world will never be the same for you."

"Never the same," he whispered.

Sirens approached in the distance as Toby buried his face in his hands and cried like a little boy.

THE OFF-SEASON

Kelli would never forgive her younger sister for this. It was bad enough that Courtney was the smart one, the pretty one, the one who did better in school, the creative one, the talented one. Kelli had grown used to Courtney outshining her in every way. All Kelli wanted was to be left alone to live her own life without hearing Courtney, Courtney, Courtney from her parents and teachers all the time.

That night, Kelli's best friend, Vanessa, was having a birthday party complete with dancing, games, and movies. All of Kelli's friends would be there. It was going to be the greatest night of the year—but Courtney ruined it.

Courtney had been invited to perform a piano concerto with a symphony orchestra as part of a holiday concert in

Atlantic City. Kelli's parents had forced her to go along and miss Vanessa's birthday party. Kelli had tried begging and pleading. She had tried making deals for good grades and doing chores, but her parents refused to give in. They insisted she come along to her stupid sister's stupid concert.

Rather than pay for a hotel, her parents decided they would all stay at her grandparents' vacation home on the Jersey shore, an hour north of Atlantic City. They arrived on a dreary December afternoon, and Kelli could see no signs of life other than a few wheeling seagulls. When Kelli and Courtney had spent summers here, the street outside was alive all day long with music and parties and fun. But most of the homes around were closed up now for the winter. This was the off-season.

Their grandparents' house sat atop stout wooden stilts, high enough that their father drove right underneath it to park the car. Kelli followed the others upstairs into the house. Her parents busied themselves making the place livable: turning up the heat, stocking the kitchen, making the beds. Courtney sat in one corner with her sheet music unfolded before her, playing an imaginary keyboard and humming to herself. Kelli seethed with bitter rage. She should be helping Vanessa set up for her party right now. Why did she have to be here? It was so unfair.

"I'm going out to the island," she announced.

Her mother frowned at her from the kitchen. "Now?" she said. "Honey, it's the middle of winter. Nothing will be open."

Crabrock Island was a great place to visit in the summer, with its endless beach, fun little shops, and

71

countless attractions on the boardwalk. Everything would be closed at this time of year, but Kelli didn't care. She just wanted to get out of the house, away from her mean parents and perfect little Courtney.

"So what? I still want to go," Kelli replied.

Courtney stopped playing her imaginary piano as their mom decided.

"Well, I suppose it's okay," she finally said, "but you have to promise to be back by six so we can be at the symphony hall in plenty of time for Courtney's concert."

"Yeah, I will," Kelli sulkily promised as she headed for the door.

"Can I come too?" Courtney asked.

"No way," Kelli answered, then hurried out before an argument could start. As usual, her mother would side with Courtney. Kelli rushed down the steps and along the vacant street, anger fueling her speed.

Unbelievable. Courtney always got her way, and now she wouldn't even let Kelli have this one thing to herself. Why couldn't Courtney just leave her alone? Kelli hated her more than anything else in the world.

THERE WERE ABOUT a dozen passengers on the ferry. Some people lived on Crabrock Island year-round, though most of the island beach homes would be closed up for the winter, and the shops, stores, and attractions along with them.

Kelli huddled by the rail, her face pressed down into her collar against the biting wind. It was colder here at the front of the boat, but the cold made her feel more alive. Plus, she had the whole deck to herself. The other passengers were inside the warm cabin or at least standing at the back, out of the wind.

The ferry was a creaky old boat, with uneven deck planks and old car tires hung over the sides as bumpers. As the engine hacked and coughed its way cross the bay, she looked down into the cold dark water and shivered.

THAT WAS THE last thing Kelli remembered when she awoke on the beach. She looked at the steely water that vanished into a foggy mist and melded into the gray December sky, but the ferry was nowhere to be seen. About a quarter mile away, she could faintly distinguish the skeletal structure of the pier and ferry landing. Behind her a string of tightly packed beach houses stretched as far as she could see in either direction.

She recognized Crabrock Island but didn't remember arriving. She recalled leaning on the rail of the ferry, gazing into the water, and figured she might have fallen asleep . . . but that didn't explain how she had wound up here on the beach.

Much as Kelli didn't want to, she decided she should return to the house, to make sure she was back by six as promised. She started to walk down the beach toward the ferry landing.

She climbed the gray timber stairs that led to the boardwalk. It seemed so broad with no other people on it.

The shacks where you could rent fishing poles or buy bait in the summer now were all closed up. She walked along the rail toward the ferry landing. The wood was worn smooth by thousands of hands trailing along it as Kelli's did now. Waves lapped at the barnacle-encrusted pilings below. As she walked, Kelli heard something splashing down there, underneath the boardwalk. Not the gentle slap of the waves against the pilings, but something more like footsteps. She stopped to listen and heard nothing. But when she resumed walking, so did the person—or *thing*—beneath the boardwalk. She glanced around at the closed-up stalls and storefronts around her but saw no one. The only sounds were the lapping waves of the ocean and the soft footsteps beneath the boardwalk.

Kelli started to run, sprinting down the boardwalk as fast as she could, but the footsteps kept following her. When she came to a set of plank steps leading down under the boardwalk, Kelli stopped. She could distinctly hear the sound of someone coming up them.

As the footsteps grew closer, Kelli was gripped with fear and started to run again. Suddenly a voice shouted, "Hey, wait up!"

Kelli froze at the sound of the voice—that horribly familiar voice—and slowly turned. It was her sister, Courtney, rosy-cheeked and breathing hard. Kelli stomped toward her.

"What are you doing here?" she demanded.

Courtney's grin faded. "Mom said I could come too. I didn't want to bug you on the ferry so I waited inside. But then . . ."

"But then what?" Kelli prompted, hoping Courtney could provide a clue to how she herself had gotten here.

Courtney shrugged. "I guess I fell asleep. I just woke up under the boardwalk a few minutes ago. I heard you walking around but didn't know who you were. Then I found these stairs and came up, and there you were."

"So you have no idea how you got here?" Kelli asked impatiently.

Courtney shook her head.

Kelli let out a frustrated sigh. "Great. You're a lot of help," she remarked sarcastically as she walked away.

"Hey," Courtney said, hurrying after, "do you know what time it is? I forgot my watch."

"No. My watch stopped."

"Well, it's getting dark. Don't you think we should go back? Mom will be mad if we're late for my concert."

"Why not? You can ruin this trip just like you ruin everything," Kelli said, not wanting to admit that she wanted to leave the island as well.

THE TWO GIRLS reached the pier where the ferry docked just as the boat was fading into the mist.

"Now what do we do?" Courtney asked.

"There's nothing we can do, unless you want to swim after it." Kelli crossed her arms and leaned back against the rail. "It won't be back again for an hour."

Courtney turned from where the ferry had vanished in the mist to her sister. "But what about my concert?"

"Too bad," Kelli said, unable to resist a smile.

Suddenly a man appeared from the mist not 10 feet away from them. Tall, grizzled, and buttoned up in a long-shoreman's blue coat, he looked menacing, but his voice sounded surprisingly gentle. "While you wait for the next ferry," he said, "perhaps you'd like to spend some time at Pirate's Pier Amusement Park. Admission is free today."

Kelli studied him. He seemed familiar, but she couldn't quite place him. She must have seen him here over summers past, she decided.

"Do you know what time it is?" Courtney asked him. "We're supposed to be back by six."

"You have time before you have to go," he told her.

"I thought Pirate's Pier was closed," Kelli said with a trace of suspicion.

The man stepped aside and pointed toward Pirate's Pier. Though the amusement park was on the other side of the island, Kelli could see a neon rainbow of lights playing against the darkening sky and hear the merry-go-round music and the rumbling of a roller coaster.

"Let's go," she said.

They crossed the island's one main street, lined with shops, restaurants, and strange attractions like the wax museum and the reptile petting zoo. All were closed.

A block past the main street stood the skeletal wooden stairway leading up to the boardwalk. Once on the boardwalk, they strolled down aisles of game booths and food stalls, sealed for the season behind sheets of canvas and weathered planks. It would have been easy to get lost if not for the guiding lights and sounds of Pirate's Pier.

Finally they reached the spot where Pirate's Pier joined the main boardwalk. While the rest of the boardwalk was dead and gray, the amusement pier was alive with colors and music. To enter, you had to pass through the mouth of an enormous skull. Its eyes were red searchlights that probed the boardwalk. Kelli had always been scared of those red eyes because at certain moments it seemed as if the skull were looking directly at her.

The ticket window was empty, so Kelli and Courtney walked right in.

"There aren't many people around," Courtney said.

"What did you expect? It's the off-season."

But the empty amusement park felt strange. As they passed the merry-go-round and the Scrambler, both rides were going full tilt, with clashing calliope music and rumbling machinery that shook the pier. But the merry-go-round horses circled riderless, and the Scrambler's spinning cars were empty.

They passed a lost-looking man with a beard and glasses and an elderly couple carrying heavy parkas.

"Do we know them?" Courtney asked. "They look kind of familiar."

"Of course we don't know them," Kelli told her. "But, yeah, they do remind me of something, I just can't figure out what," Kelli admitted with hesitation.

"Hey, let's go on the Ferris wheel," Courtney exclaimed.

Kelli allowed herself a little smile, remembering the first time she had taken her sister on this very same Ferris wheel. "You sure you're not scared?" she needled.

"Nope," Courtney said. "Not any more."

There was no line, so they walked right up and were ushered into a car by a tall, grizzled man with a pipe clamped between his teeth. Kelli thought he might have been the same man who invited them to Pirate's Pier, but before she could double-check, the wheel was in motion. Kelli's stomach seemed to fill with helium as the car curved back and upward. Both girls gripped the metal bar across their laps.

"Do you remember the first time we rode this thing together?" Courtney asked.

"Yeah." Kelli smiled as they continued to rise. "Mom and Dad's friends came for the weekend and brought their obnoxious kid—what was his name?"

"Um . . . Desmond."

"Yeah, that's right. Desmond the Demon."

"He was so mean," Courtney said. "Remember how he kept throwing food over the side of the pier, trying to get all the cats to jump off after it?"

"Yeah, what a jerk. And then Mom forced us to bring him here to the boardwalk."

"That was so funny when we lost him," Courtney said, and the sisters shared a grin. "You wanted to go on the Ferris wheel so he couldn't find us, but I was scared. I thought that the seat wouldn't turn with the wheel, that it would turn over instead and dump us out."

Kelli nodded, "I remember." Here, where it had happened, the memory seemed so fresh.

"But you said you would hold my hand," Courtney continued, starting to choke up, "and no matter what happened, you wouldn't let go. And you didn't. You held my hand the whole time, and I wasn't scared anymore."

Kelli felt tears starting to form but resisted them. When they reached the top of the Ferris wheel, it stopped, leaving their car swinging. Because of the mist, they couldn't see much besides the hazy lights of the rides below.

"You know the great thing about this place?" Courtney said. "It's always just you and me. We do everything together when we're here. The rest of the time, well, sometimes it doesn't feel like we're even still sisters."

Kelli shrugged. "I'm surprised you noticed. You're the one who's busy all the time, with music lessons and school and everything."

"Even when I'm home you never want to do anything with me anymore," Courtney pointed out. "You didn't even want to come to my concert."

"It's not that I didn't *want* to go. I didn't have any choice. Mom and Dad made me come."

"That's not my fault," Courtney said.

"Yes, it is!" Kelli shouted. "You're their little favorite, and you know it. You always get your way—always!"

"Not always!" Courtney said, her voice quivering. "I told them not to make you come to the concert, because I knew you would take it out on me. You're always so mean to me. Why?"

"Because you deserve it. You always have to have your way, and you always get it. Like now. All I wanted was to get away by myself. Could I have that one little thing? No! You had to tag along and ruin it. I'm mean because you ask for it."

Courtney broke down in sobs. Kelli could barely understand her when she said, "All I wanted to do was spend time with you, like during the summer."

Kelli stared at her little sister. Courtney covered her face with both hands as she continued to cry, and Kelli felt tears on her own face. Maybe their parents did favor Courtney, but was that really Courtney's fault? No, she realized. She thought about how horribly she had treated her little sister. All along, Courtney just wanted to spend time with her and be more like real sisters.

"I'm sorry," Kelli said.

Courtney lowered her hands and looked at her sister. "Really?"

Kelli nodded. "You're right. I have been mean to you, and you don't deserve it. The fact is . . . I'm really proud of you. And maybe a little jealous. And even if Mom and Dad do treat me differently, I shouldn't take it out on you. I promise I won't be mean to you any more."

Courtney hugged her, and they both cried until the wheel jerked into motion again. The girls gave small shrieks in chorus, and then they both laughed, tears streaking down their faces.

WHEN THEY REACHED the bottom, they had to let themselves out of the Ferris wheel seat. The man who had fastened them in was gone.

As they walked away, Kelli said, "I've got an idea. If we wait for the next ferry, we may be late getting back for your concert. So let's find a phone and call Mom and Dad. They can drive down to the bridge and pick us up. Then we can go right to the concert from there. It'll save time."

Courtney, relieved, started to relax. The two girls found a bank of pay phones by the entrance. Kelli fished a quarter out of her pocket and picked up the receiver on the first phone, but it was dead.

"This one's broken too," Courtney said, checking the second.

They checked all six phones, and none of them worked.

"Maybe they shut them down during the off-season," Kelli said, but it seemed unlikely. She was about to suggest they look elsewhere when the lights on the Ferris wheel went out. The merry-go-round slowed to a stop, its calliope music drawn and distorted before dying as it, too, went dark. Lights winked out around the pier until the girls were left in dim shadows. The boardwalk creaked beneath their feet.

"Let's find a phone somewhere else," Courtney suggested.

Before Kelli could agree, shadowy figures shambled out of the darker areas of the park and moved toward them.

"It's time," one of them moaned.

Kelli grabbed Courtney's arm and they dashed through the exit and along one of the aisles. Kelli looked back and saw the elderly couple, the bearded man, and others emerging from Pirate's Pier. They all wore an odd expression, and their unblinking eyes seemed to be focused on the two girls.

Kelli looked forward just in time to avoid running into a massive man in a football jersey.

"It's time," he said. His deep voice seemed to come from all around them.

Screaming in unison, the girls ducked to one side and past a block of shops locked up behind sturdy metal gates and curtains. Kelli saw the sign for Clarence's Crab Hut, where she and her family enjoyed fresh seafood every summer, but the restaurant looked as if it had been condemned, its doors and windows covered with sheets of plywood. At the next corner, Kelli darted in the direction of the ferry landing.

But they were soon lost in the boardwalk's maze of worn planks and plywood. Several times they saw the shadowy figures moving like zombies toward them and they were forced to change their path.

Finally they emerged from a narrow aisle to find a flight of timber stairs leading down to the pavement. They descended, but as they reached the street, something stirred in the darkness beneath the boardwalk and a voice hissed, "It's time."

The girls bolted up the block to the main street and then along its length to the ferry landing. Kelli hoped that the ferry had returned, that there would be lights and people all around, that their strange pursuers from the amusement park had ended their chase.

The ferry was sitting at the landing. And there were people there, more than she could have imagined. Firefighters and paramedics rushed about. Newspeople spoke into television cameras. And most unexpectedly, Kelli and Courtney's parents were there, huddled together and crying.

"What's going on?" Courtney asked.

Kelli shook her head. "I don't know."

They ran up to their parents.

"What's wrong?" Kelli asked. "What are you two doing here?"

But her parents did not respond. They did not even look up when she spoke.

"They can't hear you," a gentle voice said.

The old man with the pipe stood there quietly watching them. But he no longer seemed frightening to Kelli. She suddenly felt calm. The bearded man walked past, ignoring them as he stepped to the gangplank onto the ferry. The man in the football jersey and the elderly couple followed, and Kelli suddenly realized why they had seemed familiar: They had all been on the ferry that afternoon. And the old man in front of them was the captain.

"What do you mean?" Courtney asked him. "Why can't they hear us?"

"It's time," the captain said.

"Time for what?" Kelli asked.

"Sometimes," he explained, "it's hard to remember what's really important. Sometimes you have to be reminded of those things that really matter in life . . . and afterward. It's time to go."

He gestured to the ferry. Kelli felt herself drawn onto the ferry as if gently guided by unseen hands, and her mind started to clear. The mist around them drew away like a curtain. Under the night sky, the water of the bay was black, except in one area halfway to the mainland where it appeared to be on fire. Looking closer, she saw several emergency rescue boats with flashing red lights. Flaming debris drifted on the water's surface.

Memories came flooding back of when she had been standing at the rail earlier that afternoon. She recalled the way the deck of the ferry had trembled and bucked as the engine made a desperate, strained sound—a sound that ended in the explosion that had ripped the old boat apart. A giant hand had seemed to lift Kelli through the air with great power and gentleness, carrying her before she slammed into the cold water of the bay, into a darkness that engulfed her completely.

"We're dead," Courtney murmured next to her as the ferry glided away from the dock and their parents.

Kelli nodded. "We have been, ever since we woke up on the island."

The mist shifted and twisted and then formed a dark tunnel. The ferry headed into it.

"Kelli, I'm scared."

"Me too," Kelli said. She held out her hand.

Courtney took it. "Promise you won't let go?"

Kelli gave Courtney's hand a reassuring squeeze. "I promise. No matter what."

ISLAND OF TERROR

The wind blew blustery and cold, tousling Ken's shaggy blond hair as he stood at the boat's rail. He held his new 36 mm camera ready in both hands, one finger on the shutter button. The Pacific shimmered steel blue and gray under the morning sun. JJ was chasing Dennis around the deck. He had shaken up a can of soda and was threatening to open it in Dennis's direction.

"Stop that running!" Ms. Prinze, their science teacher, yelled.

Dennis stopped next to Ken. JJ wouldn't dare open the soda and risk spraying Ken. But as Dennis slid into the rail he jostled Ken's elbow. Ken fumbled the camera, accidentally hitting the shutter button.

"Hey!" he yelled. "Watch what you're doing. The only thing that kept my camera from falling into the ocean was my camera strap." He carefully examined the camera for damage and was relieved there were no scratches. He turned to Dennis. "This camera is brand-new, idiot. I got it for my birthday and if anything bad happens to it, something *very* bad is going to happen to you."

Dennis held up his hands and apologized, "Sorry, sorry." JJ stood smirking, lightly shaking the soda. He was the only kid in class who was taller than Ken, but he was much skinnier. They were both on the basketball team and hung out a lot together. Dennis couldn't play sports because of his asthma, but Ken suspected the real reason was his weight problem. Ken and Dennis had grown up only two houses away from each other and had always been best friends.

"Get any good pictures yet?" Dennis asked between gasps. He was out of breath just from JJ chasing him around the deck.

Ken knew what Dennis was doing. He was trying to change the subject so Ken would forget to be mad at him, but this new subject just worsened his mood.

"No," he said bitterly. "What am I supposed to take a picture of? The water? I could flush the toilet at home and get the same picture."

JJ snorted laughter. Dennis replied, "Well, you'll get a chance when we see some whales. Don't worry. They're always here."

"I'm not worried about that," Ken insisted. Every spring his class at school in Northern California took this field trip to see the gray whales migrating north to Alaska for the summer, and they hadn't missed spotting the creatures yet. "But if I see them, that means *he'll* see them too."

He nodded across the deck to where Tran carefully adjusted the focus of his camera. Ken couldn't even guess what their Vietnamese classmate was taking a picture of.

"So what?" JJ asked.

"So," Ken explained with little patience, "Tran won the *Daily Mirror* photography contest for our age group last year—and the $200 prize. I didn't have a chance against him with my crummy camera, but I have a shot this year," Ken said as he held up his new camera. "But it's still not fair. He gets all his stuff for free, plus he gets his pictures developed and gets expert advice for free, all because of his dad's camera shop. If we both take pictures of whales, who do you think is going to win?"

Ken stared at the waves lapping at the side of the boat, angry about how unfair everything was. He knew he'd have to get a picture of something extraordinary, something no one else had a picture of. But what?

He couldn't wait around for something to happen; he needed to find something. "Come on," he said. "There's got to be something interesting on this boat."

Led by Ken, the boys followed a gangway down into the ship. The varnished wooden steps led downward into a big open space that despite the low ceiling reminded Ken of a classroom. Chairs with built-in desk arms were bolted to the floor, facing a long table. Behind the table was a blackboard covered with a variety of maps and charts showing the migration routes of whales.

A couple dozen students and parent chaperones sat in the chairs, listening to the captain speak. Ken remembered him from last year, a burly man about 60 years old wearing a green sweater that bunched around his neck, making him look like a turtle. His captain's hat was perched on his head at a crooked angle, and he sat on the long table as if it were a bench, gripping its edge with both hands. Ken thought about taking a picture of him and almost instantly decided not to. Too boring.

The captain was in the middle of a lecture. "Take the giant squid, for instance," he said. "Huge squid, hundreds of feet long. People thought it was just a legend. But whalers found evidence. They caught whales with sucker marks—marks as big as dinner plates. People still didn't believe, not until the day one of these monsters of the deep washed up dead on a beach somewhere. No one has ever seen a live giant squid, but we know they're down there. Just because we haven't seen a creature doesn't mean it doesn't exist."

When the captain started to talk about rumors of a tribe of crab men living in the rocky California cliffs along this very stretch of coast, Ken snorted in disbelief. But part of him was thinking a picture of a crab man would win him first place in the *Daily Mirror* photo contest.

Ken's thoughts were interrupted by shouts from up on deck. As everyone moved to the stairs, all Ken could think about was that whatever it was, Tran was up there taking a picture of it. He pushed and shoved his way through the crowd heading up the narrow stairway. Once on deck, he stood on a bench to get a better view over everyone clustered at the port rail.

Just whales, he realized with disgust. Their rubbery humped backs rose from the water, blunt flippers flailing before going back under. Ken snapped a couple of pictures, but he knew he'd never get his winning shot this way. He looked over at Tran, elbows braced on the boat's rail, snapping picture after picture. Tran isn't going to win with whale shots either, he comforted himself. Whale watching was popular around here, and dozens of people probably submitted photos of whales for the contest. Yet he still wished he could just pick Tran up by the belt and toss him over the rail.

"Ken, get down from there right now," Ms. Prinze commanded from the other side of the boat.

She was standing with a couple of the chaperones and the captain at the rail on the other side of the boat. The captain had his hat off and was gesturing with it at something in the distance. Curious, Ken stepped off the bench and wandered in that direction to eavesdrop.

"I'm telling you," the captain insisted, "I've been fishing these waters since you were all as young as those kids over there, and there has never been an island here before."

Ken leaned over the rail to get a better look. Sure enough, ahead of them on the starboard side was a small island growing larger as they approached.

"ISLANDS DON'T JUST spring up overnight like mushrooms," Ms. Prinze informed the captain. "You must be mistaken."

"Why, sure," the captain replied, a little too sweetly, "maybe we headed the wrong way when we left port and that's Australia over there." Then he turned and looked up at the bridge above the main cabin. "Casey! Take us in for a closer look."

The crewman waved in response, and the captain returned his attention to Ms. Prinze. "I've always wanted to see Australia."

Preventing Ms. Prinze from arguing further, some of Ken's classmates gathered around, impatient to ask her something.

"Ms. Prinze," Missy Maxwell said, "something's wrong with the whales."

Ms. Prinze looked as if she thought the whole world were going crazy. "What do you mean?"

"You told us in class that the whales travel south to where it's warm for the winter and then go north to their home in Alaska for the summer."

"Yes?" Ms. Prinze replied, a hint of irritation in her voice.

"Well, it's almost summer, so those whales should be going north to Alaska, but they're not. They're going south. They're going the wrong way."

"I'm sure you must be mistaken," Ms. Prinze said, heading for the other rail. "It's easy to confuse directions at sea. . . ."

But Ken knew that wasn't true. With the California coast easily visible to the east, it was simple to figure out the rest of the directions. Ken saw that Missy and the others were right—the whales were swimming south.

"I don't understand," Ms. Prinze stammered. Then she looked around wildly. "I'll have to ask the captain. Perhaps he can explain this odd behavior."

But the captain had gone up to the bridge. The boat picked up speed as it veered toward the island, and Ken staked out a good spot by the starboard rail. He adjusted his camera, thinking a mysterious island might make for a prize-winning photograph. But as they moved closer his hopes sank.

As islands went, this one was not very exciting. Its rocky shores rose up to a ridge that ran its entire length, which didn't even measure a mile. The island appeared to be completely barren of plant life or houses or any other buildings.

JJ and Dennis joined Ken at the rail as they passed a few hundred yards offshore. They stared at the island for a few moments, and then JJ started pointing wildly and shouting, "Over there! Over there!"

Ken aimed his camera and peered through the viewfinder, but the barren slope was empty.

"Where?" Dennis asked. "What is it?"

"Over there," JJ said. "I thought I saw Gilligan."

He hopped out of reach, howling at his own joke. Ken lowered his camera and growled with disgust. "Do that again and you'll be looking at my fist," Ken growled.

Before JJ could respond, the whole boat lurched and shook. A horrible groaning sound filled the air. Ken fought to keep his balance on the shifting deck by grabbing the rail with one hand and clutching the camera protectively against his chest with the other. Was it an earthquake, he wondered? Could you even have an earthquake on the ocean? Dennis had both pudgy arms wrapped around the rail. JJ stumbled around and then fell on his butt. He rolled over and rode out the rest of the tremors with his skinny arms and legs spread out like a starfish. Ken would've enjoyed laughing at him if he hadn't been so scared himself.

A few seconds later the trembling stopped. Replacing the loud groaning was a whining sound from beneath the boat's deck. Ken could feel the vibrations through the soles of his shoes.

"Shut down the engine!" the captain shouted as he ran to the back of the boat. "Shut it down!"

Though she was trembling, Ms. Prinze immediately started counting heads and making sure everyone was okay. When the captain came striding back toward the bridge, she stepped directly in his path.

"What happened?" she demanded.

"Looks like we crashed into some submerged rocks," he told her. "Shattered our propeller. That was the whining sound you heard: the drive shaft turning with no resistance."

Ms. Prinze huffed, "So how do you propose we get back to port, Captain?"

"Casey," he called up to the bridge. "Drop anchor and call the coast guard. Tell 'em we've got a boat dead in the water, full of schoolkids who need a ride back to land." He looked back at Ms. Prinze. "That answer your question? Now get your kids lined up. With a hit like that, we're probably taking on water. Just to be safe, we'll ferry the kids in the lifeboats to wait on the island."

"Yes!" Ken said, high-fiving Dennis.

JJ stood up cautiously, as if afraid the boat would start to shake again. "What are you so happy about?"

"We're going to the island. There's got to be *something* there I can take a picture of. And look!" He pointed to where Tran was carefully packing his own camera gear into its case. "He's not even going to have his camera ready. This contest is mine!"

It was going to take a few trips to ferry all the kids from the boat to the island, but Ken cut in line to make sure he was in the first lifeboat. Dennis and JJ cut in right behind him. They climbed down the short ladder to the lifeboat the crew had lowered into the water, and then the captain and one of his crew rowed them ashore. When they reached the island, the captain got out, pulled the lifeboat up the rocky shore, and helped everyone get out. As he and his crewman prepared to row back for the next load, he warned, "Don't wander far, kids. There's no telling what dangers may be lurking around a mysterious island like this one."

"Yeah, right," Ken muttered, rolling his eyes. "What a cornball."

One chaperone had been put ashore with the first dozen kids, but he was occupied helping to unload passengers from the second lifeboat. Ken saw his chance.

"Come on." he motioned to JJ and Dennis. The slope was covered with jagged black boulders twice his height. It would be easy to slip away among them.

"No way," JJ said. "Are you out of your mind?"

Ken scowled back at him. "What's your problem? Scared?"

"No." He crossed his arms over his chest and returned Ken's scowl. "It's just stupid. What if we get lost, or hurt? I'm not getting left behind when the coast guard shows up."

"Don't be such a baby," Ken said, but JJ wouldn't budge. The chaperone was almost finished unloading the second boat, which carried Ms. Prinze. Once she got on shore, he'd never be able to slip away. "Fine," Ken said. He turned to Dennis. "Are you coming or are you going to wimp out too?"

Dennis shot a worried glance toward Ms. Prinze. "Yeah, I'm coming," he said reluctantly.

"Let's go," Ken said, strolling toward the nearest boulder. "See you, JJ—chicken of the sea."

After a few minutes of climbing through a maze of craggy boulders, keeping as low to the ground as possible, Ken stopped to make certain they had gotten away without anyone noticing.

"See?" he told Dennis. "Nothing to it. Now we just have to find something cool to take a picture of."

But that proved harder than he guessed. They wandered back and forth across the slope and found nothing except more craggy rocks.

"What is it we're looking for exactly?" Dennis finally asked as he trudged after his friend. "Crab men living in the cliffs? A giant squid?"

"That's not funny," Ken said. "I'm not leaving until I find something to take a picture of. A cave, carvings, a bird's nest—anything interesting."

As they wandered the slopes, they caught an occasional glimpse of the shore below through gaps in the boulders. A growing number of people were clustered on the shore.

"That's the last lifeboat coming now," Dennis said. "Maybe we should head back before they count everyone and miss us."

"No. Not yet," Ken answered with growing frustration.

"But this is pointless," Dennis insisted. He was breathing hard from all the walking. "There's nothing here at all."

Ken was so irritated, he wanted to punch Dennis. He knew what Dennis said was true, but he didn't want to admit it. He looked all around them and then had an idea.

"There," he said excitedly, pointing to the top of the ridge that ran the length of the island. "We'll go up there. We'll be able to see the whole island. If there's nothing worth checking out, then we'll go back."

"I don't know," Dennis replied. "We're going to get in big trouble."

"You're such a baby. Just go back. Start walking. Maybe you and JJ can have a tea party or something," Ken said with disgust.

Ken turned away and headed up the slope. Dennis followed after a few seconds' hesitation. They climbed straight up the rocky slope, and it only took them a few minutes to reach the ridge. As Ken stepped onto the narrow strip of level ground at the very top, a remarkable view opened up of the ocean and the California coast beyond. Ken was surprised that the other side of the island was a mirror image of the one they had just climbed. Filled with disappointment, Ken realized that even from this vantage point there was nothing much to take a picture of.

As Dennis came huffing up behind him, Ken raised his camera and snapped a few shots of the distant coastline.

"Find something?" Dennis said between gasps.

Ken shrugged, "Maybe. Come on." He started walking along the ridge toward the south end of the island.

"But you said after we climbed up here we'd go back."

"In a minute," Ken said. "I just want to see what we can see from the very end. It's not that far."

Ken reached the point where the ridge suddenly dropped at a sharp angle down into the ocean. Gazing down from this point, Ken could see a group of whales swimming away from the island.

"Still going the wrong way," he muttered. "Stupid whales."

"Hey, Ken, look!" Dennis said, lagging behind. Ken joined him looking down the slope to see that two coast guard ships had arrived to evacuate everyone.

"We have to get back," Dennis said, "or we'll get left behind."

"They won't leave us behind. By now Ms. Prinze knows we're missing. She won't let them leave without us. Just hang on for a second. I want to get a picture of these whales."

He went back to the end of the ridge and raised his camera. Sure, he thought, anybody can get a picture of whales, but from this high up? It made the gigantic creatures look tiny, and the unexpected perspective might impress the contest judges.

But as Ken studied the whales through the viewfinder, he noticed something odd. Though the whales were swimming directly away from the island, they seemed to be getting closer. The whales were being followed by a dark shadow in the water. Judging from the size of the whales, whatever was making that shadow must have been as big as a house. Ken's finger froze on the shutter button as an enormous reptilian head rose from the water. Its mouth snatched up one of the whales as if the huge mammal were a snack and swallowed it whole. Ken understood now why the whales were going the wrong way. They were fleeing in terror.

The surviving whales dove underwater, and the great monster submerged its head to chase them. As the beast disappeared into the cold Pacific, the whole island started to shake.

Ken suddenly realized this was no island. As the great monster dove to pursue its prey, its body began to submerge. Ken and Dennis staggered and hugged what they had believed were boulders to keep from falling. They were actually knobby growths on the monster's skin. Ken was able to see down the slope where the last boats had reached the safety of the coast guard ships. His classmates would escape with their lives. He and Dennis, he understood as the angry, churning water rushed up at them, would not.

SHELL RAISER

"One-fifteen . . . one-sixteen . . . one-seventeen," Carlos counted as he bounced the soccer ball off his left knee, his right knee, his right toe. "One-eighteen . . ." This time, for variety, he used his head to butt the ball into the air, but he got the angle wrong and it spun off across the patio, coming to a stop against his sister's wheelchair.

"Cut it out," she murmured without looking up from the video game on her lap.

One hundred eighteen was nowhere near his record—which was 207. He had been trying all morning to set a new one and now was too bored and tired to try any longer. But there was nothing else at all to do.

He walked over to where Carmen was playing her video game in the shade of a patio umbrella.

"Leave me alone," she warned, "I'm almost to the last level."

He hadn't planned on doing anything, but now he had been told not to, he couldn't resist. He put a hand over Carmen's eyes. She tried to duck her head and crane her neck to see around him, but it didn't work. Ominous electronic music announced the death of her character.

"Carlos, you jerk!" she shouted.

He smirked as he picked up his soccer ball. It was the most fun he had had all day—the most fun since they had arrived in Hawaii yesterday. Their father, a big-shot executive who was here for some important meetings, had decided to drag the whole family along. Their mother was spending her vacation time on the phone with employees at her public relations firm back home in San Diego. Between phone calls she suggested that Carlos and Carmen go play on the resort grounds, but they had beaches in San Diego, so they weren't wowed by the idea.

"Klutz," Carmen said.

Looking down the beach, Carlos noticed a group of kids about his age. They were walking along the surf with their heads down, not even talking to each other. Occasionally one would bend down to pick up something.

Carlos hesitated for a moment. He wasn't the most outgoing person in the world, but he was so bored that working up the courage to talk to complete strangers seemed almost easy. Maybe they would be up for playing soccer. Or maybe they were into Skull & Crossbones, the collectable card game he played constantly with his friends at home.

As he neared them, one of the boys looked up.

"Hi," Carlos said. "Do any of you play soccer?"

"Not today," the boy said. "Today we're looking for shells."

Carlos walked along with him. "Can't you do that anytime?"

"Yes," the boy replied as he scanned the sand, "but today Mr. Kona is coming. He buys the shells from us to make jewelry for his shop."

"Really?" Carlos said, with thoughts of Skull & Crossbones cards racing through his head. "Will he buy them from anyone?"

"Sure," the boy said with a grin. "He'll be down by the public fishing pier around four o'clock. But I don't think you'll find many. We're cleaning off the beach pretty good."

The boy's words didn't bother Carlos because he had a plan. By the time he returned to the beach with his snorkeling gear the kids were much farther along—too far to see what Carlos was up to, he thought with a smile. He waded knee-high into the surf, then put on his fins and mask. With the snorkel clamped between his teeth, he floated in the water. The sound of his own breathing filled his head as he looked for shells. All around him, the shells tumbled and danced with the rhythm of the waves. Carlos snatched them up and put them in the mesh bag as he drifted along.

He felt guilty after a while, abandoning Carmen on the hotel patio in her wheelchair. One of the few places she couldn't go was the sandy beach, but their father had taken her snorkeling late yesterday afternoon after his meetings were through for the day. He had promised to teach Carlos how to surf but spent all his time with Carmen instead. She had always been his favorite.

Once his mesh bag was full of shells, Carlos waded ashore and carried the bag and his gear back to the hotel. Carmen, still on the patio, was now reading a book.

"Where have you been?" she demanded. "What are you going to do with all of those seashells?"

"That's for me to know and you to find out," he told her.

CARLOS LET CARMEN tag along as he followed the sidewalk along the beach to the public fishing pier. A line had formed along the rail to where a gray-haired Hawaiian man sat behind a card table, examining the shells the kids presented to him. Carlos got in line with Carmen behind him, craning her neck to see what was going on.

While he was waiting, Carlos opened the mesh bag and started to sort through his shells. Most of them seemed pretty ordinary: white, pinkish, or tan shells ranging from the size of a quarter to that of a chocolate chip cookie. But a few were outstanding, including one glossy black beauty that spiraled around and around to a sharp point. He noticed the kids in line in front of him listening to their shells to hear the ocean, so he went ahead and raised the black shell to his ear.

Carmen said something, and as he turned to tell her to shut up he heard a whisper from the shell that sounded like *"Killll herrrrr."*

Carlos froze and a chill ran through him. He listened for the message to be repeated, certain he must have heard it wrong. But just then, Carmen snatched the shell from his hand.

"Ooh," she said, "I've never seen a shell like this before. It's so pretty! Can I have it?"

"No way," Carlos said, grabbing it back. "It's the best one. This shell is going to make me some serious money."

At least that was what he hoped. When he reached the front of the line, he placed the mesh bag on the table, along with a few individual shells he thought were the best, including the black one.

His eyes widening at the sight of the black shell, Mr. Kona spit out a string of words that made no sense to Carlos, picked up the black shell, and hurled it toward the ocean. Thinking the man was nuts, Carlos backed away from the table.

"I'm sorry, young man," Mr. Kona explained, his expression softening, "but black shells are bad luck. In these islands, in the past, if someone were possessed by an evil spirit, a holy man would force the spirit out and trap it in a black shell, which was then thrown into the ocean." He grinned. "I know you think this is foolish. Show me what else you have brought. I will try to make it up to you."

It looks like the black shell won't be bad luck for *me*, Carlos thought.

MR. KONA WAS true to his word. Carlos left the pier with a handful of dollar bills. After he waved them in Carmen's face, he headed for a local comic book shop where they sold Skull & Crossbones cards. He bought four booster packs, which he opened right there in the store. Hidden among the familiar cards he already had he found a rare foil-stamped Captain Sharktooth. It was one of the few he still needed to complete his set.

By the time Carlos got back to the hotel, his parents and Carmen were dressed and ready for dinner. They went down to the lobby to wait for him while he changed. After he put on long pants and a button-down shirt, he grabbed the plastic case containing his Skull & Crossbones collection. He wanted to be sure to place the new Captain Sharktooth card in a protective sleeve and file it with the other valuable cards. But when he opened the case, he found something odd.

In one of the compartments was the black seashell Mr. Kona had thrown away this afternoon. Or was it? It looked like the same glossy black spiral-shaped shell. But how had it gotten into his card case?

Carmen, he thought. She'd been there on the pier. After Carlos left she must have found the shell and hidden it in the case as a joke. He thought Mr. Kona had thrown it into the ocean, but he guessed it landed on the pier where Carmen could have reached it.

Carlos removed the shell from the case, left the room, and hurried down the hall to the elevator. Riding in the elevator, he felt an urge to put the shell to his ear, to see if he heard the same eerie message. At the same time, he sensed something warning him not to. He wasn't a superstitious person and didn't really believe Mr. Kona's story about evil spirits, but something about the shell felt very wrong. He wrapped his left hand around his right, which held the shell, and when the elevator doors opened he hurried out. Spying a trash can with a swinging cover so you couldn't see what was inside, Carlos jammed his hands through and dropped in the shell.

He looked around to make sure Carmen hadn't seen where he'd disposed of the shell. He spied her across the lobby on their father's lap, laughing. Daddy's little princess, he thought.

Carlos thought he heard a sound from the trash can, the quietest whisper. He hurried away before he could be sure.

CARLOS'S PARENTS TOOK them to a luau, complete with booming drum music and hula dancers. Torches lit up long tables filled with roast pigs, pineapple wedges, and other supposed island specialties. His father whisked Carmen out of her wheelchair and into the crowd of dancers, laughing as she moved her hands like the hula dancers.

Carlos got up to take a closer look at the buffet tables. Putting his hands in his pockets, he felt the familiar cool, grooved surface and point at one end and knew what it was before he pulled it out to look—the black seashell. Hearing Carmen's laughter over the music and excitement, he was struck by an overwhelming urge. He raised the shell to his ear.

"*She steals his love from you,*" the shell whispered as he watched Carmen dance with their father. "*Killlll herrrrr.*"

Just then, a waiter with a tray of drinks bumped into Carlos. The impact jarred the shell away from his ear. He looked down at it in horror. Not far away, a pig on a spit turned over a large glowing fire. Impulsively, Carlos stepped toward it and tossed the shell into the flames. Even squinting, he couldn't see the shell in the intense glow. He hoped that would be the end of it.

CARLOS CHECKED HIS pockets a hundred times that evening, but thankfully the shell did not return. On the way back to the hotel, he thought he saw it lying on the ground, but it was just a rock. When he and Carmen went back to their room, he hurried through the door first, looking around for some sign of it. But the shell was nowhere to be seen, not even in his card case.

Finally he started to relax. While Carmen was in the bathroom, getting ready for bed, he stepped out onto the balcony. From the 17th floor, all the lights below looked like diamonds on black velvet. Normally Carlos didn't like heights, but the rail was sturdy and the breeze light. This view was one thing they did not have at home.

Then something crashed into his knees from behind. As he staggered, something grabbed him by the belt and started to lift him. Twisting as his feet left the ground, he saw Carmen behind him in her wheelchair. Using one hand to hold him easily above the ground as if he weighed no more than a kitten, Carmen pressed the black seashell to her ear with her other hand. With a blank face she leaned forward and forced him over the rail. Carlos tried to hang on, but she was superhumanly strong. Quickly, he kicked the shell out of her hand. It flew from her grip and he dropped onto the rail. He clutched at the rail to keep from tumbling over as Carmen blinked and then looked at him with wide, horrified eyes.

"Carlos, I'm sorry," she said. "I don't know what happened."

"It wasn't you," he told her as he got his feet back on the balcony. "It was that thing." He pointed at the shell, now on the floor of their room.

Carmen looked at it as if it might leap to attack them. "It said horrible things to me. It said . . ."

"What? What did it tell you? To kill me?"

She nodded. "It said Dad loves you more, because you were first."

Carlos couldn't help laughing. "Loves me more? Don't be an idiot. He loves you more. Dancing around with you, taking you snorkeling. He hasn't spent any time with me."

She shrugged. "But he always leaves work early so he can go to your soccer games. He never takes off work to see me."

Carlos wanted to tell her she was wrong but realized she wasn't. "Okay, maybe we're both being silly," he admitted. "He's a busy man who makes time for both of us when he can. But that thing, it's turning us against each other."

"We're always against each other," Carmen muttered.

"That's not true. Sure, we argue and call each other

names. That's what brothers and sisters do. But I don't want to kill you."

Carmen snorted a laugh. "That's nice. I don't want to kill you either." They smiled at each other for a moment. Then Carmen looked back at the shell on the floor and her smile faded. "What do we do with that?" she asked.

Carlos shook his head. "I don't know. I tried throwing it away and burning it, but it keeps coming back." He snapped his fingers as an idea struck him. "Mr. Kona! He knew about the shell. Maybe he'll be able to tell us what to do. But since we can't go to see him until tomorrow, we should put it somewhere where we can't get to it. We need a safe or something."

"We could put it in my jewelry box," Carmen suggested. "I'll hide the key, and you can put the box on the shelf over the coat hangers. You won't be able to get in without the key, and I won't be able to reach the box. That way we'll both be safe."

Carlos nodded. "That's a pretty good plan. When did you get so smart?"

"I've always been smart," she said with a smile. "When did you get so observant?"

WHEN HE AWOKE the next morning, Carlos found the shell on the dresser.

"Mr. Kona's jewelry store is listed in the phone book," Carlos said after he checked. "According to the map, it's not too far."

"Good," Carmen said. "Let's go right after breakfast."

Their father had already gone to his meeting when they reached their parents' room. They went to breakfast with their mother, but within a few minutes she was on the phone with her office. Carlos and Carmen excused themselves with a wave and went upstairs. They wrapped the shell in a towel and put it in the cargo bag on Carmen's wheelchair before heading off for Mr. Kona's shop.

Kona's Handcrafted Treasures was a small building designed to look like a hut set in the shade of clustered palm trees. Inside, a glass case stretched across the front of the store, filled with rings, pendants, and tiny figurines carved from seashells.

A curtain parted and Mr. Kona emerged from the back of the store. He was smiling until his eyes landed on Carlos, and then he became grim. He nodded before Carlos could speak.

"The shell speaks to you," he said.

"To both of us," Carmen corrected him.

As Carlos pulled the towel-wrapped shell from the bag in Carmen's wheelchair, Mr. Kona gestured for them to come around the counter. He gave Carmen a friendly smile as she maneuvered her chair through the narrow space. He then held the curtain aside to allow them into the back part of the store.

The back room was several times larger than the front, with a long workbench cluttered with magnifying lamps, vises, and other tools. Boxes of assorted supplies crowded the shelves. Mr. Kona told Carlos to sit on one of the stools by the workbench. Then he went to the shelves and stretched to reach the top one. From it he pulled an old wooden box. Placing it on the workbench he began sorting through it.

"The spirit inhabiting the shell has formed a connection with you," he said as he removed jars and pouches from the box. "It will continue to plague and torment you until you accept it and free it from its prison. Then it takes control of you to pursue its own evil ends."

Carlos and Carmen shared a frightened look.

"What can we do?" Carlos asked.

"We must break that connection. Give me the shell. Fortunately for you, my grandfather was a holy man. He taught me the ways of the spirits."

Mr. Kona laid the towel on the cement floor after opening it to expose the shell. Then he opened a jar containing black powder and poured a circle around the towel. He lit a thick yellow candle and from a leather pouch poured a circle of white powder around the stool where Carlos sat and also around Carmen's wheelchair.

"Whatever happens," Mr. Kona told them, "do not leave the circle until I tell you to."

He then threw a pinch of the white powder in the flame of the candle, filling the air with a sweet white smoke. Chanting, Mr. Kona began to walk counter-clockwise around the circled shell. After a moment, goose bumps rose on Carlos's skin as another voice began a different chant. It came from the shell and quickly rose in volume. Mr. Kona chanted louder, competing with the voice from the shell until their shouted words boomed and echoed in the small space. The shell twitched and jumped like a living thing.

Finally, Mr. Kona picked up the yellow candle and held its flame to the circle of black powder surrounding the shell. Within the circle, a column of flame shot up, all the way to the ceiling. The towel was incinerated instantly, but the flames did no damage to the shop. Carlos felt no heat, even though he was only a few feet away. The shell trembled and then lay still. The flames died away. The voice from the shell faded to a whisper and finally went silent. Only then did Mr. Kona stop chanting.

"That spirit is a strong one," Mr. Kona commented. "Very evil. The two of you were fortunate to escape its control."

"So, it's . . . dead now?" Carlos asked.

Mr. Kona shook his head. "No, there is no killing a spirit. But it remains trapped in the shell and its connection to you has been severed. It has no power over you now."

He picked up the shell and walked toward the back of the shop. "Come, let us return it to where it belongs."

Carlos helped Carmen with her wheelchair as they followed Mr. Kona out the back and down a short walk to a boat pier. They went to the very end, and Mr. Kona hurled the shell with all his strength.

As Carlos watched it disappear into the sea, he earnestly hoped he would never see it again.

WHEN CARLOS AND Carmen returned to the hotel, they were pleasantly surprised to find their father looking for them.

"You two seem to be getting along awfully well," he said as Carlos pushed Carmen toward the hotel lobby.

"Dad!" Carlos said. "What are you doing here?"

"Yeah," Carmen said. "It's the middle of the day."

He grinned. "When they called a bathroom break for my meeting, I snuck out. Come on. We're going to have a picnic on the beach. I've even talked your mother into leaving her cell phone behind in the room."

Once their mother joined them, they strolled along the beach, looking for a good spot. Carmen rode on her father's shoulders. Carlos carried the picnic basket and his mother carried an armload of blankets and towels. As they walked along the edge of the surf, the water licking at their ankles, their father suddenly stopped and leaned down.

"Look at that," he said, reaching for the glossy black shell. "I've never seen anything like it."

"No!" Carlos and Carmen simultaneously shouted.

Stunned, their father turned to look at them.

"Black shells," Carlos explained, "are bad luck."

BLACKHEART'S TREASURE

"Never dive off the left side of the boat," Manuel said. "Always the right. People who dive off the left side—sometimes they don't come back."

John nodded gratefully to the smiling first mate and started to walk across the deck of the slim sailboat. His rubber flippers slapped against the wood and made him clumsy, like some water bird not used to walking on land.

"Walk backward," Manuel advised. "It's easier."

Even though Manuel's advice didn't make sense, John tried it. Sure enough, Manuel was right. John wasn't so sure about the rest of his advice—not to dive off the left side of the boat—but he figured better safe than sorry. John realized he didn't know much about snorkeling or sailing, and so far Manuel's advice had all been right on the mark.

John reached the right side of the boat and checked his mask and snorkel to make sure they wouldn't pop off when he hit the water.

"Merry Christmas!" his father called.

John smiled over his shoulder at his father, who reclined in a deck chair at the back of the boat in the shade of the sail. He held a fishing pole but seemed to be more interested in trading fishing stories with Captain Dorney, who was sitting on the rail nearby. Behind Captain Dorney and his father, John could see the beach of the tiny deserted island a few hundred yards away.

"Merry Christmas," echoed John's mother. She and his twin sister, Lynn, were both sunbathing at the front of the boat.

"Merry Christmas," John replied, smiling at the confused look on Manuel's face.

"It's February," the crewman said, shaking the dreadlocks out of his face. "How come you all think it's Christmas?"

"This trip was our Christmas present to one another," John explained. "We had never been on a real vacation before, so my mom and dad gave us this trip to the Bahamas and no one got any presents this year."

"I see. Then Merry Christmas to you." Manuel nodded his understanding and added, "Don't touch anything down below. If it's pretty, it probably stings."

More good advice, John thought, filing it away. He stepped off the side of the boat and plunged into the sapphire blue water. He surfaced, rinsed out his mask, and then lowered it over his face. With the snorkel mouthpiece clamped firmly between his teeth, he let his head sink under again.

The ocean shut out all sound except for its own muted hum and the magnified rasp of his breathing through the snorkel. The blue-tinged reef stretched away from him into the hazy distance, alive with a thousand living creatures—swaying sea anemones, tiny white crabs, a sand-colored ray, and fish in all sizes and colors. Some fish traveled in schools like shimmering silver clouds, while others, such as a two-foot barracuda that hovered in the water for a moment and then vanished in a burst of astonishing speed, prowled the reef alone.

John idly kicked his flippers and drifted over the reef. Everywhere he looked he could see the most amazing ocean life. When they were discussing where to go on their chartered boat, Captain Dorney had highly recommended this island. He explained it was deserted and far enough away from other islands that tourists avoided it. But the snorkeling, he claimed, was the best in the world. Now that he had a chance to see for himself, John believed him.

John was disappointed that no one else in the family was interested in snorkeling. His dad would much rather see a fish on the end of his line than face to face. His mother didn't enjoy swimming, and Lynn had said that snorkeling was "lame." She didn't say why and John figured she was just sulking. Yesterday, their first day in the Bahamas, she and her mother had gotten to choose the family's activities, which had involved a morning of shopping and renting mopeds for a tour around the island. Neither he nor his father had enjoyed it much—the shopping was boring, and John's moped got a flat tire on the far side of the island. But John didn't think that he and his father had complained nearly as much as Lynn and his mother were doing today. Lynn had kept her nose in a book all day, and John's mother kept grumbling about how much chartering the boat was costing them.

For John, the peace and tranquillity beneath the surface of the water was the best part of his vacation so far and a welcome change to the griping and sulking on the boat. He studied every inch of the reef and was rewarded with glimpses of sinister-looking eels peering out from their lairs and fish that looked so much like parts of the reef that John almost missed them. This encouraged him to carefully examine every inch of the reef.

Passing slowly over the reef's far end, John noticed a strangely shaped outcropping. It wasn't gracefully curved like most of the reef but instead was composed of straight lines. As he studied it further, he realized it wasn't a natural outgrowth of the reef, though it had been there so long that coral and barnacles had grown over it. Once he recognized what it was that he'd found, a wave of excitement shot through him. He burst out of the water and spit out the snorkel mouthpiece.

"Hey!" he shouted, waving at the sailboat. "Hey! I found a treasure chest!"

CAPTAIN DORNEY HAD a little motorboat on board that they used for going ashore in areas too shallow for the sailboat.

He, Manuel, and John's dad motored over to where John floated above the reef, flushed with the excitement of his find. Manuel stripped off his shirt, put on a pair of goggles, and joined John in the water. John held his breath and dove down to show him the chest. It took five dives and a hammer to get the chest loose from the reef. It was too heavy for Manuel and John together to haul to the surface, so they attached a rope to one of the iron handles on the side and towed it back to the sailboat. They then used the pulleys for raising the boat to hoist the chest out of the water and onto the deck.

John's mother and sister joined them around the chest. To open it, Manuel worked with a screwdriver, scraping off the barnacles and other growth that covered it. Now visible were the old oak chest's ornate iron bindings and hinges as well as its hefty iron lock. And finally, on its top, a plaque engraved with the name *The Sea Reaper*. Manuel looked alarmed.

"Well, I'll be," said Captain Dorney. He was a portly man about the same age as John's father. He wore a tattered Hawaiian shirt and kept a pipe clamped in his jaw most of the time, though John had yet to see him light it.

"What is it?" John asked. "What's wrong?"

Captain Dorney gestured at the plaque with his pipe. "*The Sea Reaper*—she was captained by William Faulcon. Blackheart, they called him. When he plundered a ship, he killed everyone on board. Men, women, children—it didn't matter. They used to say his heart was blacker than the bottom of the sea at midnight. Go on, Manuel. Open her up."

Since they had boarded the sailboat this morning, this was the first time John had seen Manuel without a smile. But the first mate did as ordered and returned his attention to the chest. He pried at the lock with the screwdriver until the brittle metal snapped. Then he forced open the lid, the hinges groaning like living things. John was amazed to see that it really *was* a treasure chest! The damp gold coins gleamed in the sunlight. And mixed among the coins, like prizes in breakfast cereal, were gems and pieces of jewelry.

Lynn gasped and snatched up a ruby pendant on a gold chain. John picked up one of the coins and turned it over in his hand, feeling its weight against his palm.

"Yahoo!" his father shouted, holding up a jeweled gold cup as if making a toast. "We're rich!" He turned to John. "Do you know what this means?"

"Vacations all the time!" his mother said.

"Vacations from our vacations!" his father said.

Lynn put on the ruby pendant and admired her reflection in a cabin window. Captain Dorney was inspecting the stones set in the hilt of a silver dagger. John's mother tried on a jewel-encrusted bracelet. Only Manuel had yet to touch any of the treasure. He squatted next to the chest, his face expressionless.

"What's wrong?" John asked him.

"This Captain Blackheart," Manuel whispered. "You know what happened to him? The widow of a Spanish captain whose ship he plundered, she put a curse on his treasure. Whoever possessed it, she said, would be plagued by bad luck and tragedy. After that, Blackheart and *The Sea Reaper* disappeared. No one ever saw them again."

John looked at the coin in his palm. A chill shot up his arm and down his spine. He threw the coin back into the chest and shivered in the hot sun.

Captain Dorney removed the pipe from his mouth and laughed. "If I were you, folks, I would worry less about curses and more about the authorities."

John's father stepped closer to the captain, crossing his arms over his chest. "What do you mean?" he asked.

"If you take this treasure back with you to the Bahamas, the government will lay claim to it, and you'll not have a dime for your trouble. On the other hand, if you were to offer my first mate and myself half the contents of this chest, we would be more than willing to smuggle you into Florida. There you could sell your half of the treasure for millions and keep all the proceeds yourselves."

John's mom and dad drew away together, but he could still hear them discussing the captain's offer. "Half the treasure is better than no treasure," he heard his mom say.

When they rejoined the group, Lynn protested, "We have to go back to the Bahamas. All our stuff is there."

Her father smiled at her. He tapped the pendant she wore around her neck and said, "This will buy us *new* stuff." Then he returned to the chest full of gold and jewels. "Captain Dorney," he said, gazing at their newfound riches, "take us to Florida."

AN HOUR LATER they were heading west in the open sea. John watched as his mom and the captain sat in the shade,

looking on as Lynn and their dad sorted the treasure and counted coins. Manuel seemed to be the only other one who had doubts about the treasure. John joined the first mate at the helm of the boat.

"What are you going to do with your share?" he asked.

Manuel shook his head as he guided the boat. "I don't want any share of what's in that chest. The rest of you, you're welcome to all of it."

"Don't you want to be rich?"

Manuel laughed, his smile returning for the first time since the chest had been opened. "Who says I'm not already rich? Besides, Captain Blackheart, he owned the whole chest. How do you think it ended up on the reef? It seems to me being rich didn't do him a whole lot of good."

This made perfect sense to John. All the money in the world wouldn't do you much good if you weren't alive to spend it.

"So what do you think we should do with the chest?" John asked.

"Throw it back. Let the sea be rich."

John glanced over to where Lynn was parading around the deck, with rings on every finger and bracelets up to her elbows. His parents and Captain Dorney were laughing and clapping. They would never agree to drop the treasure back into the ocean.

As he watched his sister twinkling with gold and gems in the sunlight, he remembered Manuel's earlier warning: "If it's pretty, it probably stings." Manuel hadn't been talking about treasure, but he might as well have been.

THAT EVENING THE captain set out a seafood feast to cele-brate their good fortune. They dined on lobster tails, steamed clams, and sea bass filets smothered in lemon juice and butter. The captain prepared the food in the galley and served it on deck, with sparkling grape juice for John and Lynn and champagne for their parents.

After dinner, they told stories and laughed until the sun went down. That was when they started to get sick.

"I don't feel good," Lynn said, her hands clasped over her stomach.

A few minutes later John felt it too, a clawing pain in his belly as if some spiny creature were stirring angrily in there. His parents developed symptoms soon after.

"Too much seafood, I guess," the captain said. "It can hit you like that if you're not used to it. I'll check below for something to make you feel better."

After he had gone, John overheard his mom mutter to his dad, "Don't you think it's strange how only we are affected? Not Manuel or your buddy the captain?"

His father shrugged. "They're used to the food."

"I don't know. I didn't see either of them eat very much."

"What are you saying? You think they're trying to poison us?"

She glared at her husband and replied, "All I'm saying is that starting tomorrow, I'm not eating anything I didn't cook myself."

THE NEXT MORNING, John awoke in a hammock on deck and was surprised to find the ship not moving. The sails were raised but hung slack from the mast without even the slightest breeze to stir them. The water was like glass, stretching smoothly and unmoving to the horizon. Banging and rattling sounds came from the rear of the ship, so he headed in that direction.

John found Manuel sitting by an open hatch. The sounds he had heard were coming from down there.

"What's going on?" John asked.

Manuel held up his arms, gesturing all around them. "No wind. No go."

"Does this happen very often?"

Manuel shrugged. "Sometimes, but according to the weather services, our sails should be full."

John felt a growing dread in the pit of his stomach. "It's the curse, isn't it?"

Manuel shrugged again. "You have to make up your own mind about that. All I know is, the sails are empty when they should be full, and our auxiliary motor, which was serviced just last week, doesn't want to start."

Captain Dorney's head appeared through the hatch. "There's nothing wrong with that motor as far as I can tell." He heaved himself up onto the deck and wiped his greasy hands on a rag.

"So what do we do now?" John asked.

Captain Dorney sighed, gazing out over the still sea. "We wait," he said.

BY THAT EVENING, the wind promised by the weather service still had not arrived. The rest of John's family passed the time playing cards, using the gold coins to bet with, but John would have nothing to do with it. He didn't want to touch anything that had come out of the chest.

He and his family still felt weak, with occasional stabs of stomach pain. The captain, he noticed, was now pale and trembling, and Manuel sweated as if in the grips of a fever.

Dinner was a plate of canned beans each and a small stack of crackers, a far cry from last night's sumptuous feast.

"Yuck!" Lynn said. "I hate beans."

"Sorry, dear," her mother said as she handed out the plates. "There wasn't a very big selection."

"We only laid in supplies for one day at sea," the captain said. "We weren't expecting to be out this long. We have only a few canned goods left, but they won't last us another day." He paused, clearly working up to saying something important. "I think we need to put that chest overboard."

Manuel nodded firmly, but John's mom and dad and Lynn cried out in protest.

"Not a chance," his dad said. "We have a deal, Captain. You're taking us and that treasure to Florida. Big deal—so we've had some bad luck with the weather."

"And sickness," Manuel said.

"And the motor," John added.

His dad glared at him. "But that's no reason to get all superstitious. There's no such thing as a curse. That treasure's staying on board. I know none of us is feeling too good at the moment, but next week when we're all rich you'll be glad you listened to me and stuck it out."

Captain Dorney, apparently, was convinced otherwise. When John and his family got up the next morning, the captain, Manuel, and the small motorboat were all gone.

"THOSE FOOLS," JOHN'S dad muttered, scanning the sea for some sign of the motorboat. Then he ran to check the treasure to make sure they had not taken any of it with them.

John shook his head. He knew the treasure would all be there. His father still did not understand.

"What are we going to do now?" John's mom asked.

His dad closed the treasure chest and stood. "We're going to Florida," he said.

"And who's going to sail the boat?"

"I am. I've been watching Dorney and Manuel. It doesn't look too hard." He put his arm around John's shoulders. "How about it? Want to be my first mate?"

John shook his head. "I think we should throw the treasure overboard."

"No way!" Lynn said.

His father scowled and removed his arm from around his son's shoulders. "I can't believe I'm hearing this."

"Let's at least radio for help," John's mom implored.

"No! If the authorities come, they'll take away our treasure. Doesn't anyone have any faith in me? Sailing's not that hard. Look, there's wind again today. All we have to do is point the boat west and we'll hit land. Probably sometime today. It can't be much farther."

His dad was right about the wind, but John still had doubts. Apparently, his mother did too, because after his father went to the helm to steer the boat, she ducked into the cabin. John followed and caught her frantically twisting the dials on the radio.

"It doesn't work," she whispered, her eyes filling with tears. "It doesn't work."

John hugged her and told her everything would be all right. But he didn't really believe that himself—not as long as Blackheart's treasure was on board.

As THE DAY progressed, the wind not only held but grew stronger, with blustery gusts that snapped the sails and blew John's hair every which way. This improved his dad's mood, but by late afternoon they had still not seen land. Dark clouds started to appear, massing overhead and turning the sky black. The sea turned an ominous gray as the waves picked up strength, lifting the sailboat high and then dropping it, like a roller coaster.

John's dad still manned the helm, but John, Lynn, and his mother took shelter in the cabin with the chest. Waves swept across the deck outside and tossed the boat as if it were a toy.

John's mother stared at the chest. At first he thought she was scared of it, afraid to take her eyes off it just in case it opened and released some further misfortune on the family. But as her eyes grew narrower and her face became stern, he realized she wasn't frightened—she was angry.

Finally she stood against the rolling of the boat. "Help me, John. We have to get rid of this thing."

"No!" Lynn cried. But John ignored her as this was the chance he'd been hoping for. He jumped up and grabbed one end of the chest while his mother snatched the other. The chest was incredibly heavy, but they managed to drag it across the floor to the few stairs leading up to the deck. Lynn ducked past them and out into the storm, headed for her father.

John and his mother didn't waste time with words. They both grabbed one handle and dragged the chest up the stairs, straining to get it up on deck. It took all their effort. Lynn and her father waited for them on deck. John and his mother looked at them defiantly.

"It's no good, Tom," John's mother told her husband. "It won't do us any good if we're all at the bottom of the ocean."

He stared at them a moment, until a wave struck the side of the boat. They all stumbled and staggered, and Lynn clutched her father to keep from being swept overboard.

He nodded to his wife. He grabbed one end of the chest, while John and his mom took the other, and together they wrestled the chest to the edge of the boat. Lynn ran after them, pleading for them to change their minds, but they did not hesitate. The chest tumbled over the side and disappeared into the black water.

John's father told them to get back inside while he returned to the helm. Soon after, the storm started to break up. The waves ceased their abuse of the sailboat, and as the ocean calmed, the exhausted family fell into a deep sleep.

"THE RADIO WORKS!" John's mom shouted as she bolted from the cabin the next morning. "The coast guard is sending a ship for us!"

John smiled in relief. His father, at the helm of the boat, was grim-faced and quiet. He struck the wheel of the boat several times in frustration. Then he resumed his silent staring.

"What's wrong with him?" John asked Lynn as she skipped by with a stack of crackers. "And why are you in such a good mood?"

"He's mad about throwing the treasure overboard," Lynn said. "He thinks he panicked during the storm and let you and mom talk him into it. Now he's thinking about all the money he's lost."

"Oh," John said. He felt bad for his father. Not only did they not get the money, but their hard-earned vacation was pretty much ruined. Still, he thought, at least they were alive to complain about it.

Lynn hummed merrily as she nibbled a cracker.

"And why are you so cheerful?" John asked her.

"Because I'm the smart one in the family," she told him. She reached inside the collar of her shirt and showed him that she was still wearing the ruby pendant. "I didn't let myself get all crazy like the rest of you over some stupid curse."

John stared after her as she twirled away, wondering if they were all still cursed or if his sister alone would have to suffer. He had a bad feeling they wouldn't have to wait long to find out.